The G

Princess R Lakshman

The Girl Child
Princess R Lakshman

Price: AUD $ 24.95
: NZD $ 26.99
: INR Rs. 450

ISBN 978-0-473-11673-6

Cover designed by Adarsh Auchraje © 2006
Printed by G.Olivannan, Emerald Publishers, Chennai, India

For
Pauline Mascord

> "Oh Lakshmi, Goddess of wealth
> I pray to you to give me riches
> Not misfortune, nor poverty, nor ill-health
> I pray to you to give me sons
> No daughters, no, none"
>
> — Anonymous

> *Kudhiye meri desh diye*
> *Takdeer banale tu*
> *Tere te koi zulm kare*
> *Talwaar utha le tu*
>
> — Mangal Hathur

Translation

> *Girls of my nation*
> *Make your own destiny*
> *Should injustice befall you*
> *Seize the sword for your protection*

Princess Reineeta Lakshman, born in 1975, is a Fiji-Indian. She is a Natural Therapist and a freelance writer on the areas of natural health and travel. Her articles have been featured in *Healthy Options Magazine, New Zealand Fitness Magazine,* and *Travel Digest.*

Inspired by real life events, *The Girl Child,* is her first novel. She is currently working on her second novel and numerous feature article assignments. For more about the author, visit her website:

www.thegirlchild.com

Acknowledgments

I thank the following people for being my source of inspiration in many aspects of my life. Some of you have contributed towards this book directly and most of you indirectly. Your help, well wishes, guidance, prayers and unconditional friendship I will forever be indebted to. Thank you …

Ganpati Bapa…may you continue to remove obstacles that come into our lives. Bapu ji…sat naam sat guru maharaj. My family…Sethi, my soul mate, without you this book may not have been. Komal, my darling daughter, I love you more than anything in this whole wide universe and beyond and back. My parents, you nurtured me and allowed me to spread my wings and fly…I love you both, unconditionally.

My teachers at Rampur College and Yat Sen Secondary, Fiji - Mrs Shakuntla Anchraje, for instilling the love of literature in me. Mrs Tejinder Kaur, you made me fall in love with Punjab back when I didn't even know where Punjab was. Ms Sarita Prasad, when no one else wanted to care, you nudged me on to remember my oratory speeches, thank you. Mrs Mere Young, for your brilliant guidance and affection. Mrs Bessie Ali, for letting me be part of Yat Sen Secondary.

My dearest friends… Tamsin Calder, you are the epitome of true friendship, love you. Yasmin Haq, my astrological twin, never a day goes by when I do not think of you. Dr Margaret Mishra, when I'm down, your phone calls cheer me up, your wisdom inspires me. Adarsh and Soniya, God bless you both, thank you for the mind-blowing cover. Jane Darnell, the only one who truly manages to put in words my inner thoughts, Jane, thank you for being such an amazing woman. Farhana

Farook, physically we are many miles apart but you are and will forever have a special place in my heart.

Geoff Brennan, my mentor during a critical phase in my life, you're an inspiration. June Keir, for your ever encouraging words and guidance and for being the first one to read draft number one. Brian Morris, David Pardon and the entire team at NZIBS, for your encouragement and support.

And finally, thank you to all the writers whose books inspire me everyday: Amulya Malladi (thank you for your emails), Chitra Banerjee Divakaruni, Vikram Seth, Manju Kapur, Enid Blyton, Sidney Sheldon, Hari Kunzru, Rohinton Mistry, Monica Ali, Jhumpa Lahiri, Cathy Kelly, Maeve Binchy, Marian Keyes.

Chapter One

The Waiting Game

District Hoshiarpur, Punjab, India 2002

It's peculiar how a pregnant woman's tastebuds behave. If someone had asked me to eat cauliflower or eggplant curries a couple of months ago, I'd have given them a "Bugger off" look. But today I crave spinach saag with vast quantities of melted homemade desi ghee (clarified butter), tandoori roti, and a glass of chilled yoghurt lassi. Oh yum!

I lie on my bed fantasising about these sumptuous dishes, waiting for the appropriate moment to go downstairs to satisfy my cravings.

The ceiling fan revolves incessantly, groaning like a chakki wheat grinder with gravel-infested grains. I stare at it, hoping for miracle answers to all the questions buzzing in my head about the months to follow. As much as it's fantastic news to know I'm pregnant, the reality of what's to come is at times overwhelming. In less than eight months I'll be a totally new person and I'll have a little person who will be entirely dependent on me for everything. Everything!

As I lie thinking about the world of babies my thoughts keep getting interrupted by the noise coming from downstairs - the usual daily gossip session between my mother-in-law and her sister-in-law. Boy, do they carry on! Do they ever give up? I mean so what if Ram Singh's daughter-in-law only wears inauspicious white salwaar kameezes despite being a married woman, or Bagga's wife doesn't cover her head in public, or Pinky, the temple cleaner-girl, always leaves behind some dirt under the door mat? No one gives a hoot except these two.

Outside is not the only place where the constant chattering is coming from. I hear the groans in my stomach, complaining about missing the breakfast I had silently refused this morning. Silently it was indeed. No one noticed. Not even Gurveer.

Lately he's been giving all his attention to Papa-ji, Gurveer's father, and their business trips. I thought at least Gurveer would be on my side during this special phase in my life. Our lives. But nah. Off he went on his Hero Honda bike. Going to the sabzi mundi - the fruit and vegetable market - he told me.

He was angry when he left this morning. No, not with me, with Bi-ji, his mother and Bua - his father's younger sister. He too is fed up with their daily gossip sessions every morning.

It starts dead on ten o'clock when Bua comes in through the front entrance gates, bringing with her a stench from the shrivelled rupee notes she keeps tucked under her kameez in the breast area.

Bua and Bi-ji have an unusual relationship. When they're not together they indulge in bitching about one another and when they are together which is from ten a.m. till midday almost daily they indulge in bitching to each other about everyone else.

Didi, wife of Gurveer's elder brother Jasveer, had warned me in my first few days as a new bride that I must keep personal details to myself. I got on fabulously with Didi and Jasveer from the moment I met them at Delhi airport. Being three years older than Gurveer, Jasveer loved it when I addressed him as Pa-ji, the respectful Punjabi term for older brother. Didi's proper name is Paramjeet but the respectful term for her is Didi, elder sister. Gurveer addresses her as Bhabi-ji, sister-in-law.

"These old hags love to drain all kinds of personal information out of people and then tell the whole mohalla about it," Didi had warned me.

This is why Gurveer and I are still toying with when and how we'll tell his family about our big news. The news that will change my life forever. Our baby news.

We had started trying for a baby since our wedding night, actually the night after. Traditionally the newly wedded Punjabi couple must not consummate on the night of their marriage since legend has it that if the couple makes love on their wedding night the groom will face death in the very near future.

Naturally I slept with Didi that first night. The hilarious thing was they all knew that Gurveer and I had been sleeping together from way back in Auckland, but just as every other traditional custom had been followed, so was the no-sex-on-the-first-night one.

The wait was fun and sexy though. Our room was nicely decorated with rose petals, a tray set out with sweetmeats and almonds, and there was a tall glass of milk on the bedside table for Gurveer. "Make sure he drinks the whole glass," Didi told me before we were taken into room that smelled like a rose garden and shimmered like a sari bazaar. "It'll make him perform with flying colours."

I felt like telling her that her not-so-innocent brother-in-law always performed with flying colours.

I was allowed in the room first so I could sit on the bed with my face under the veil for Gurveer to lift up. Later Gurveer's female cousins and other younger women guests pushed him into the room with shrills of school-girl giggles.

From that night we had desperately wanted a child. Often when we lay in each other's arms on the manjah - a bed made out of a steel frame with interwoven ropes - on the rooftop terrace outside our bedroom, we gazed at the stars and wished for a baby.

It took ten months for the stars to grant us our wish.

Four weeks ago we went to the medical clinic for a blood test for typhoid fever. For four consecutive days I had noticed a slight fever which lurked into my body at around midday and stayed there for a few hours and Papa-ji had said it could be typhoid fever. This was a possibility as I was no longer on the Bisleri bottled water but had started drinking tap water, unboiled.

Since my cycle was two weeks late that month I asked the pathologist to do a pregnancy test as well. Gurveer and I didn't know whether to laugh or cry when the smiling young girl at the clinic told us I was pregnant. We tipped her a hundred rupees, which she accepted graciously, confirming that I didn't have typhoid fever after all.

We decided to keep the news to ourselves for the time being. Gurveer got us an appointment for the next day to see Dr Siddhu, a pot-bellied obstetrician who wore a turban twice the size of his head, to find out all about what to expect when one is expecting. Amidst our secret elation was the silent issue we both dreaded.

Since our wedding day every single person in the Choudhary clan had been blessing me to have a son. Not once had anyone mentioned the joy or even the normalcy of having a girl. The one person who was always on my case was my mother-in-law. Every. Single. Time. On and on Bi-ji went about how Wahe Guru would bless her youngest son with a handsome son soon!

"How do you think Bi-ji will react if it's a girl?" I asked Gurveer at Dr Siddhu's clinic the next day.

"She'll be overjoyed, I know that much...but you

know how she is."

"Why does this have to be so hard? I wish she didn't have to be this backward." I fidgeted with the end of my duppatta.

Gurveer squinted and placed both his pointing fingers on the bridge of his nose, a pose he always adopted when in a dilemma. He finally spoke. "Well, I guess it's just that she's illiterate and old-fashioned and superstitious. And Bua doesn't help either."

I could taste the bitter medicine smell that wafted in the waiting room of the clinic. The white walls began to move closer towards me. My lips struggled to form the words to go on speaking but I had to.

"I think I know what we can do," I said, gazing hopefully into his clear hazel eyes.

"What?"

"What if we just tell Pa-ji and Didi for now? And maybe tell Bi-ji and Papa-ji after the first three months has passed, when it is safe," I blurted out without realising I'd gone a little too far.

"When what is safe?" He moved his fingers away from his nose rest and placed them on his chin, his elbows digging into his thighs. His knees shook rapidly, like the misaligned steering wheel of a car, as he balanced his weight on his lifted heels.

Trying my best not to sound accusing, I answered, "When...when Bi-ji can't force me to get rid of it..if it's a girl."

There, I had said it. Gurveer glared at me. I knew that look. I had seen it many times before. The time he didn't know how to tell his parents he was in love with me - a girl who though Indian but not born in India. A girl who was Hindu not Sikh. A girl who was Gujrati not Punjabi, and whose three previous generations had been born and bred in Fiji, not India. A girl who had later spent most of her life in a white man's country and was not the typical Punjabi daughter-in-law type. A girl who knew no divisions of caste - and who was not a Gujjar, a member of the cowherder caste that Gurveer's family and forefathers were.

Yes, I knew that look. That same confusion. That same fear of a possible loss. His eyes, hazel and as clear as a freshly cleaned swimming pool, indicated that he was just as concerned.

I had suggested that we tell Pa-ji and Didi first because I knew he trusted them. And they were the ones who had actively supported his decision to marry for love. The first love marriage to ever take place in the Choudhary dynasty.

I took a deep breath hoping the sound my sigh would make him look at me. He continued ignoring me, pretending to read the notes on "Breastfeeding is Best for Mother and Baby" that was pasted on the wall next to him.

"You hate me for saying that, nah? I love Bi-ji, you know that. But what if…" I was afraid to voice my fears.

"Don't think like that," he said.

"I'm scared, Jaanu." I only called him that when I wanted to show him how much I loved him.

"Fine, then we'll do what you said. We'll tell Pa-ji and Bhabi-ji tonight when Bi-ji and Papa-ji and the children are sleeping."

I nodded my approval and gave him half a smile. He turned around on his seat to face me and stroked his thumb gently across my cheekbones. I realised then that I had tears rolling down my face.

He cupped his hands around my face and kissed my forehead. "Priya, meri jaan. I love you so very much. This is our creation and we will do whatever we must to protect it," he assured me.

I loved it when he called me his jaan, his soul.

Later that night we shared our big news with Didi and Pa-ji. They knew exactly how we felt. Harpreet, their daughter, whom everyone affectionately nicknamed Preetu, was their first-born and so they could see in us what they'd gone through six years before.

"Your Didi went back to her parents' home to give birth," Pa-ji told us. "I came home with armloads of takeaway curries from Ambar Restaurant. To celebrate. Bi-ji and Papa-ji were sitting on the manjah outside. Lakshmi aaii hei, Goddess of wealth is here, Lakshmi aaii hei, I had told them. But they only gave me a horrified look and didn't utter a single word."

"That's so unfair. Hasn't Preetu brought us prosperity since she was born? Indeed she has been our little Lakshmi. Look at how our dairy farm business has flourished," Gurveer said, disgusted with his parents' behaviour.

"Arre mere bhai, I know, I know. But you should have seen their faces at that moment. I was so angry I took all the food and fed it to the municipality dogs. At least the dogs would have given me blessings for feeding their hungry stomachs."

"Pa-ji, didn't you say something to Bi-ji and Papa-ji about how unfair they were being to you and Didi and Preetu?" I asked, fear invading a section of my throat.

"Priya, of course I asked them about it the next morning, when I sobered from all the whisky the night before."

"What did they say?"

"What they always say...Lakshmi aaii nahi, Lakshmi jayegi - wealth has not come to us, wealth will be taken from us."

Terrified, I looked at Didi in consolation. "And what did you say, Didi?"

"Priya, be strong. I would pray that Wahe Guru Ji gives you a son first," she replied, as though in a hurry to hide the truth about her feelings.

"How can you say that Didi? Aren't you happy that you had Preetu first?"

"Of course I am. More than anyone can ever understand. But what followed after Preetu's birth was unbearable for me, Priya. There were always demands for a boy. Your Pa-ji is the oldest son in this house and someone has to carry the Choudhary name forward. Thank God I had Ranveer two years later. I don't know what I would've done if I'd another girl instead of Rannu."

My chest began to feel heavy. It wasn't so much anger as disgust I felt with Didi's ignorance, her submissiveness. She sounded just like my mother at that moment, and I wondered if Ma had felt disappointed when I was born because she too had been hoping desperately not to have a daughter for the second time. Though disappointment was probably a much nicer word I susepected Ma had felt hatred at the first sight of me. Maybe if I'd been a boy Ma and Pappa wouldn't fight so much and would love each other the way all my friends' parents loved each other.

Gurveer gently placed his hand on mine to calm my fingers that were murdering each thread of my chiffon duppatta tassel. He looked at Pa-ji and Didi.

"We don't want Bi-ji and Papa-ji to find out until a few months have passed. Will you both swear not to tell them? Please?" Gurveer begged.

"Gurveer, you are like Ranveer to me," Didi assured him. "Have your Pa-ji and I ever let you down? Don't worry, we're always with you and Priya."

Gurveer got up from his seat and touched his bhabi-ji's feet, a tradition he had assumed from the day Didi came into this house. The older brother's wife is like a mother to her young brother-in-law - a tradition aptly depicted in the Ramayana epic where Rama's younger brother Lakshmana worshipped Sita, Rama's wife, as his mother and promised to tackle all evil before it ever touched her.

Despite boasting about the richness of values from such renowned epics, the Indians don't shy away from forcing younger sons to marry their bhabi-ji in the event of death of her husband. A young man, once taught to worship his sister-in-law as a son does his mother, is then shamefully ordered to take her as his wife and produce the next generation.

"Jinda reh, pooth, go on living, my son," Didi blessed Gurveer.

*****

My stomach grumbles as I continue staring at the ceiling fan. I realise that sooner or later I'll have to eat something even if I end up spewing it out minutes later as I've been doing for the past couple of weeks. I'm glad our bedroom is upstairs. Gladder that Gurveer and I have our own private bathroom. Every morning for the past fortnight I've eaten my breakfast only to trudge up the stairs to the bathroom for a regurgitating session.

I'm careful not to let Bi-ji notice these daily episodes. Women in this part of the world seem to smell pregnancy from a village away. She's too smart to let it pass as a minor tummy bug which is what I keep telling Tara, our housemaid, though I suspect even she will soon make out heads from tails.

It's almost impossible not to run into Tara each morning on my sprint to the bathroom. She would either be mopping the upstairs terrace floor at that precise moment or folding Gurveer's kurta-pyjamas that he always leaves scattered around on the bedroom floor the night before.

Sometimes she would just be staring at my photos in the turquoise mirror-rimmed picture frames. There is one with me in my grey bridge-climbing suit waving from the top arch of the Auckland Harbour Bridge. Another shows Gurveer and me at Devonport ferry jetty, all rugged up on a winter's day. And then there's one with me, Ma, Pappa and Daksha Aunty at Daksha Auntie's fiftieth birthday bash in Queenstown.

Tara isn't the usual maid-type. She's smart and bubbly, and curious about the Western world where she knew I spent most of my teenage and adult life. Tara comes from a respected family. She's proud of her tenth standard education and when I first entered Choudhary Niwas, Gurveer's parents home, as a newly wed, asked shyly,"Memsahib, you Australian, nah? I see them always on TV, playing cricket. They always thrash our desi boys. Will you teach me English, please Memsahib?"

She was a cricket junkie and adored the Aussie team. It took a good half hour for her to grasp that I was in fact a Kiwi and not an Australian. At first she was disappointed but I cheered her up when I told her that Kiwis also played cricket and were equally good at it if not better sometimes. She had grinned with excitement and begged me again to be her English teacher.

"On one condition," I told her.

"Haan ji, ki?" Yes, what is it?

"That you'll call me Priya."

"Nonono, nahi baba. Aa gal theek nahi, not good idea. I work for you. I am servant. You are Memsahib. Choudhary saab ji is my master."

"But they pay you, right?"

"Haan ji. Always on time. Three hundred rupees every month on the fifteenth."

"Well then, Tara, that makes you our employee, not our servant. You and I are equal, okay?"

"Memsahib, please don't talk like that. You will get into trouble from Choudhary saab ji. But you know, he is good man. Only Bi-ji too much talking sometimes."

We formed a silent friendship almost instantly. Tara agreed that every day after she'd finished her chores she would come into the hall room upstairs for her English tuition.

It's always fun exchanging Bollywood gossip and cricket updates with Tara. She is seldom keen on her fellow "desi" Indian cricketers as she thinks they spend too much time doing TV commercials and not enough time practising the game, which according to her is what they really should be focussing on. She also objects to the unchanging order of play. "Give the new boys a chance. Always the same order - Tendulkar, Dravid, Ganguly, hai ram, I'm sick of it already." The only time I see her a little patriotic is when India plays Pakistan.

I respect Tara for her strength and stamina to go on with life the way she does. If there are any sorrows in her world she certainly won't let them get in the way of her living it up. And sorrows there are, which I came to learn a couple of months after getting married.

On that particular day Tara had suggested I put henna in my hair. I had just had lunch and was sitting on the upstairs terrace outside my bedroom. Gurveer had gone to Himachal Pradesh with Papa-ji to sell a truckload of cattle. Papa-ji bought these cattle at a quarter of the price from Hoshiarpur's smaller villages. Rannu and Preetu were at school and their daddy-ji had gone to his best friend Mintu's motor garage to meet his mates for their daily matka betting.

Didi and Bi-ji were lying on the manjahs on the porch downstairs. They had two hours to nap before it was time to return to the dairy farm behind our two-storey home for the afternoon shift. Every morning at four and every afternoon at two-thirty Didi and Bi-ji milked our forty-seven cows. The milk was then sold to selected commercial halwai sweetshops in Hoshiarpur town and to many residents as well.

Ramu and Raju, our dairy farm help, were snoozing in their servant-huts built next to the dairy farm. Ramu's job was to clean and feed the cows and Raju's was to pour the milk into six twenty-litre tin cans then load them onto his bicycle to make the deliveries to our loyal customers.

The September autumn sun danced on the beige terrace floor tiles as Tara parted my hair at different sections. She had insisted putting the henna on my hair herself even though it was her time to go home.

As we chatted about the usual hair and beauty tips she proudly revealed her age. "Thirty-five, Memsahib," she told me, the glow of her turmeric-golden skin defying this confession. She looked twenty-two at most.

I realised she was the same age as my older sister Pouja. Yet there was a vast difference in their maturity - like the taste of dhal and kadhi - both yellow but one grainy and spicy, the other milky and mellow.

Tara's glass bangles clinked as she dabbed her curry-stained fingers into the bowl to scoop out the henna paste. Having finished the hair on the back of my head she proceeded to the crown area. It was a relief to relax my neck back into its straight position after the strain of holding my forehead down for what seemed like hours. With my head up, I once again marvelled at the kaleidoscope of colours reflecting from Tara's bangles, playing hide 'n' seek on my light blue salwaar kameez.

"Tara," I said.

"Haan ji, Memsahib?"

"Tara, tell me about you. About your family. You never talk about yourself. C'mon, tell me, nah?" I usually adopted a casual tone when we were alone, though since Bi-ji despised the idea of being friendly to the hired help I hardly spoke in this manner to Tara when Bi-ji was around.

"Well Memsahib, I am like dust on furniture. My life is so boring, not like Kylee Minuug's." (She took Channel-V interviews way too seriously. I often translated these interviews to her and there'd been one episode with Kylie Minogue, bless her).

After much pestering she told me a little about herself, wearing a brave face and her never-failing Promise toothpaste smile throughout her tale.

I discovered Tara has two daughters, Jyoti and Maya. Though she comes from a middle-class family, she married for love to a lower caste boy and as a result her parents disowned her. Her only sister passed away two years ago from tuberculosis. Being the angel that she is, Tara agreed to adopt her sister's child because her sister's husband and his family didn't want to bring up a daughter. Instead, a mere few days after being widowed, Tara's brother-in-law decided to remarry.

Tara ignored her drunkard husband's protests and brought home her four-year-old niece, Meenaxi, to live with them. One day her good-for-nothing husband took all her jewellery and sold it."Memsahib," Tara said, "the bhen-chodh, the sister-fucker lied to me. He said he needed the jewellery to start a business so we could save for our daughters' dowries. Months went by. No business. Nothing. He stayed home only. Sipped his lassi and listened to Punjabi FM on his stupid transistor. Then ekdum, very, very suddenly, he became very polite with me. Didn't even force himself on me at nights. But Memsahib, it was all a trick. He'd used the money to pay this agent in Jallandhar for a visa to Canada, and now he was days away from getting it. Then one day, after I came home from my jhaadu-pocha, mopping-brooming job, I found a note on the table under his transistor, telling us 'Bye-bye - going to Canada'. My youngest daughter, Maya, was only two."

I listened with disbelief. What a selfish bastard. How could Tara remain so courageous after suffering for so long?

She was almost done with putting the final strokes of the green, mint-smelling paste on my fringe when I turned suddenly to face her.

"Arre Memsahib, be careful you'll ruin your salwaar suit." Tara jerked her hands back.

"How long has it been since he left you, Tara?"

"Fourteen months."

"Are you sure he's in Canada?"

"Haan ji, Memsahib. He sent two thousand rupees from there one month after he left. Since then, nothing. No more news. Maybe in Canada, maybe Umrikka, don't know."

It was difficult for me to comprehend what my life would be like if Gurveer walked out on me like that. I'd never be able to talk to anyone about it as casually as Tara could. I would have spent days and nights crying but Tara was strong. She came to work, earned an honest living for her daughters and niece, learned English in her spare time, and managed to laugh. I had always admired Oprah Winfrey for being a woman of substance but hearing Tara's story made me wake up and smell the coffee that India's villages were full of women of substance. Women who had the courage and determination to withstand anything, absolutely anything, life threw their way.

I was overcome with a mixed feeling of sadness and pride. I wanted to cry at that moment. And I also wanted Tara to cry. To let out all the anguish she'd been suppressing behind her brave smile. I wanted to tell her it was okay, that she didn't have to put on a smile for our sake.

Then I realised that maybe she did cry when she was all alone on her side of the bed. Was she alone in her bed? Or did her daughters share it? Or maybe another man? Well, if not in bed then maybe she cried in the shower.

How brave of Tara to go through such a mess and still be interested in who scored the highest runs in cricket tests. How different I was from her. Back home, if I had even a trivial problem I used to be on the phone to Tammy, my best friend. Tammy did the same. She'd ring me on my mobile and say, "Let's go to Robert Harris for a cuppa. I'm a total mess. Jake and I broke up." Or sometimes it was about someone she was pissed off with at work, or a fight she had had with her mum, or even something as silly as "I hate my body!" which was a fairly common one we both liked to use as an excuse to gulp down more sticky date puddings with ice-cream and caramel topping (our favourite).

I was just as bad. I'd call her at work or send her text messages on her mobile phone and bitch about my father and his teeny-bopper girlfriends, or Pouja and her crazy sicko boyfriends who hated my guts. "Gotta talk. Meet me @ Ponsonby," my text would read.

I wondered if Tara had any girlfriends to pour her heart out to. Probably not. Who would she tell anyway? Every woman I'd met in this city so far seemed to be disguising their sad marital truths with heavy make-up, jewellery, and expensive salwaar kameezes. Sort of like my Ma who always found something nice to say about my Pappa to her women friends, the only friends she was allowed to have.

I turned around to face Tara again. Nothing I could say would heal her wounds. I decided to embrace her bravery and not say anything.

Several silent minutes passed before my Gemini "good communicator" personality took over, yearning to comfort Tara and tell her how amazing I thought she was and how I could never measure up to her strength. I wanted to say something, anything. Any old cliché would have been fine - Tara, there's always tomorrow, or There's plenty of fish in the sea, or even, it's better to have loved and lost than never to have loved at all.

These clichés would have worked with Tammy but not with Tara. With Tara it was so damn difficult, almost as difficult as telling a child the little floating goldfish in the bowl isn't sleeping, it's dead, or that Santa Claus isn't real.

"I have another slang for you today, Tara," I finally managed to say. She liked using Kiwi and Aussie slangs, especially "G'day mate".

"Really, Memsahib, what is it?" she asked, excited.

"When we are proud of our female friends back home we say, 'You go, girlfriend'."

I hugged her tight so she couldn't see my tears.

The warmth of her cheeks on mine reciprocated my intention but she didn't hug me back in case her henna hands spoiled my salwaar kameez.

"Tara, you go, girlfriend," I whispered in her ears.

Tara smiled back weakly, her lips trembling slightly. She knew exactly what I was implying.

*****

The gossip downstairs seems to have died down. Bua must have left because I can hear Bi-ji snoring on her manjah in the porch.

Gurveer is still not home. Didi has gone for her Shahnaz Hussein Gold facial appointment at Himani's Beauty Parlour. It isn't likely she'll be back for another few hours, knowing chatterbox Himani ji, whose one-hour appointments usually end up lasting for three.

I figure everyone else is either out or snoozing so it's safe to go downstairs. I get up from our king-size bed-box. Funny things these bed-boxes. "You sleep on top and keep your saris down below," the salesman had told me in his best possible TV-commercial voice, during our furniture shopping. Hmmmm, very practical, I thought, a sleep-on storage box.

I place my feet on the floor only to jerk them back up from the cold marble tiles. From under the bed I pull out my camel-coloured leather jootis to slip my feet into. My hair is a knotted mess but I can't be bothered to comb it so I tug the black scrunchy from my bangle-clad wrist and pull my black mane into a lazy bun.

Walking over to the dressing table I gaze at my reflection in the almirah mirror next to the dresser. I had expected to see sagging bags of flesh under my eyes and a dull face from several weeks of restless nights. Instead I'm greeted with a glowing complexion. I'd always splurged loads of money on all sorts of French skincare products from Farmers and Life Pharmacies but could never manage to glow like this. If being pregnant means having skin this beautiful I'd like to be pregnant forever.

In a circular motion I run my fingertips over my face, starting from my forehead, chin, and then back to my forehead. My skin feels smooth, like whipped cream. I look into my eyes. Someone once said your eyes are windows to your soul. My pea-sized baby is my soul. I wonder if my little bub can see her mother...or his mother. I gently place my palms on my belly. Slightly twisting my waist, I stand to face the mirror to get a side view of my belly. It isn't a bump quite yet. I smile and whisper,"Hi, you in there."

I stare at myself for a few more seconds, with a unique awareness about my body. The kind of awareness you feel when doing the sav asana, the meditative yoga pose.

My thumb reaches for the fan switch on the pale blue wall next to me. Click. The chakki groan slowly fades away. Only the flip-flap of the burgundy tie-dyed Jaipuri curtains and the tick-tock of my side table clock remain. It's one-thirty. Definitely time for pet-puja, stomach worship.

Bi-ji's snores become louder as I descend the eleven steps that separate my upstairs sanctuary from the downstairs world of bickering, daggy old women's kutch-kutch and puk-puk. If it wasn't for the kitchen I'd probably happily spend the next eight months in the comfort of my room and our terrace, so large I've never seen one like it in Auckland - not even in the *Designer Homes* magazines. But sadly vaastu shastra, Indian feng shui, didn't allow Choudhary Niwas to have an upstairs kitchen. Damn.

I tiptoe past Bi-ji into the spotless, spacious

kitchen adjoining our living room. Stainless-steel plates arranged immaculately, lie face down on the emerald-green marble-top counter. Matching steel tumblers, also face down, stand on top of each plate. Didi is adamant about these details. She supervises when Tara washes the dishes. "Tara, aise nahi aise." Not like this, like that, she would say.

I ladle my plate with aaloo-gobhi and two rotis and fill my tumbler with lassi, adding two teaspoons of sugar to it. It's almost two o'clock and there's usually a good soap on TV at this hour.

India has to be the only country to have cable TV for such a small price. Sometimes no price at all if one knows how to tangle a few wires here and there to steal the cable channels. Like our Jasveer Pa-ji does.

I begin surfing channels to find something worth watching. Sony, DD-Metro, Sahara, Zee, HBO, Star….finally settling on *Kumkum - Ek Pyaara Sa Bandhan* an emotional soap on Star Plus. It revolves around the main character Kumkum, which literally means the red powdered dot worn by women on their forehead as a sign of marriage. In today's episode poor Jatin, Kumkum's husband, is dying of cancer taking his last breaths in the oncology ward. The red bridal kumkum bindi on Kumkum's forehead is going to be wiped off forever, to symbolise her widow status.

I am sucked into Kumkum's world like millions more who have tuned in to watch. My mouth chews and swallows each bite and my eyes moisten with each morsel of emotive language that Jatin uses on his deathbed to tell his father how much he loves Kumkum. Like me, Kumkum has a little one growing inside her belly.

But like all TV soaps, just when things begin to gain momentum an irritating commercial takes over the screen.

This time it's cricket sensation Harbhajan wrestling with a cheetah for a chilled Pepsi. Being the Coke lover that I am, I use this time wisely and get up to wash my hands.

Aah, nothing like a full stomach. *Hi, you in there, hope you enjoyed the aaloo-gobhi.* I pat my belly softly.

After a while Kumkum becomes way too emotional to keep watching so I switch to Channel-V where Shakira thrusts her hips and swings her belly in her "Whatever Whenever" hit number.

It isn't long before the comfort of the Rajasthani block-print settee sends me off to la-la land.

When I eventually awaken, Ranveer is halfway through his Punjabi composition homework and Harpreet, as usual, is fumbling with the TV remote, channel-surfing.

"Pooth, why didn't you wake me?" I rub my eyes and let out a dreary yawn.

"Ssh Chaachi-ji, don't disturb please," Ranveer scolds. "Madam-ji will make a murga of me if I don't get this stupid composition finished." It's common practice for teachers to punish children by making them squat and twist their arms through their bent knees to touch their ears, commonly known as the murga pose.

"Rannnu, mind your language," Harpreet jumps in. "Chaachi-ji, kya hei ki, the thing is, we decided it was good for you both to rest for as long as you wish." She gives me a little wink.

Harpreet is old enough to know I need plenty of rest but poor Ranveer has no idea what she is talking about. "Chaachi-ji, Preetu hasn't even finished her homework. Kal dekhna, tomorrow Madamji will make murga of her." He pokes his tongue out at Harpreet and pretends to flap his arms like a chicken.

These kids give me a renewed energy each time I'm with them. It's a joy to be part of their innocent world. Actually I lied before. It's Rannu and Preetu who compel me to come downstairs. Bi-ji and Didi's voices float in from the outside kitchen where they always cook roti on the earthen stove. Looking at the wall clock above the TV I realise it's almost five o'clock already. My mouth has been shut for a couple of hours and I can smell a bit of garlic breath from my lunch earlier. I decide to freshen up before dinner. The kids, engrossed with their usual puk-puk, don't see me leave to go upstairs.

Opening the door to our room, I smile in relief to find Gurveer fast asleep with the razai half covering his thick black curly hair. Hesitant at first, I walk towards him. Meri Jaanu. How I missed him all day. I wonder how long it has been since he returned home from the sabzi mundi. Or wherever else he went to drown his dilemmas.

I kiss him softly on his stubble. He opens his eyes with quick sudden blinks, his mouth opening and shutting as though sucking on his tongue, like a goldfish.

"It's only me, my Jaanu," I whisper, my lips softly kissing his ear.

"Missed you...so much," he mumbles, half awake.

He always knows what to say. With the pregnancy my emotions have been like a roller coaster. I cry so easily nowadays, for no reason or sometimes for reasons too hard to explain.

His words bring tears to my eyes. At times I feel so out of control. Being a typical Gemini I like to have my feelings, actions and reactions under control. But I guess I have to get used to the little one growing inside me. The little one who has already become the centre of my universe. And who now holds all reins of control in my body.

Gurveer pulls me towards him and kisses me on my neck softly at first, and then as I reciprocate, his passion intensifies. He begins undressing me in an unhurried, careful fashion. His hands pull each garment of clothing off me with extra care, not wanting to hurt our baby in any way, especially not in this way.

It has been almost three weeks since we last made love. He positions himself on top of me and slides his lips on my neck. His kisses are wet and fervent. I run my fingers through his hair and stroke the back of his neck, then his chest, then finally when I can't take it any more I place my hands on his firm buttocks and guide him inside me. Long ecstatic minutes eventually transcend into an eruption of a simultaneous orgasm. Exhausted from the pinnacle of pleasure we lie in each other's arms.

"Hungry?" he asks, my head resting on his chest.

"Famished!"

"Great, let's go out."

"Wow, really? I mean, are you sure - is it going to be just you and me? Like back home?" My tone is like that of a child who's just been told she has a ticket to Disneyland.

"No, actually there's one more person coming," he replies in a somewhat serious tone.

I spoke too soon, I realise.

Grinning, he says, "Silly, I'm talking about our little bub." He places a kiss on his palm and caresses my bump-less tummy with it, transporting the kiss to his child.

I wrap my arms around him tightly and say, "Oooh, that sounds fabulous. I think I'll wear my Esprit jeans then. Where are we going? Or is that a surprise too?"

"I was thinking...how about Haveli?"

"We can't drive all the way to Jallandhar - what will your folks say?"

"They'll say something only if they know something, nah?" He raises his eyebrows and gives me a mischievous grin. His sexy, cheeky grin. "C'mon, no one has to know, yaar. You get changed while I go and tell Bhabi-ji we're going to the doctor for the regular check up. She'll handle it. Now hurry before I eat you all over again, you hottie. Has anyone told you you're even sexier now then ever?"

"Chaddo ji...Jaanu, you're crazy." I give him an affectionate push before he attempts to prove his manhood again.

"Yes, crazy in love, with you two!"And after another little peck on my naked belly he leaps off the bed to work on our eloping plans.

God only knows how much I've been longing for us to escape for some couple-time. Living in Punjab, thousands of miles across the seas from Auckland, had been my decision and I'm loving every moment of it too. But when it comes to alone-time with Gurveer I really miss our usual city hangouts.

We called them our ab fab - absolutely fabulous - places: Mission Bay, Ponsonby, Devonport, The Hare Krishna Temple at Riverhead and our number one spot almost every Friday night was the little Italian restaurant in Parnell. The best pasta in town.

Back then we could just get up and go without worrying about offending any members of the extended family. Not that we had any extended family living with us. I was too smart to let him move in with me in my quirky Patel family. So it was just me and him in our one-bedroom place in Howick overlooking the bay.

Couples rarely did that in Punjab. Live together before marriage, I mean. Even after marriage hardly any family is nuclear unless the son gets his job posted out of town. Here in Punjab families live together. And pray together, eat together, laugh together, cry together, gossip together, fight together and if one giant bed was possible they'd probably all sleep together (not in any incestuous way though!). Passionately ostentatious Punjabis.

So you can see why it's so hard for couples to have their alone-time in such situations. It is almost always a given that when a couple announces they're going out (meaning just them!) the entire household jumps up with joy and hurries to get changed, much to the couple's disappointment, which of course goes unnoticed by anyone else in the house. Why? Simply because no one would be left standing there to notice the couple's grumpy expressions - everyone else would be halfway into their best salwaar kameezes by then or struggling to fit their over-sized turbans through their kurtas.

Chapter Two

Sands, Pebbles and Rocks of Time

Gurveer was the first in his entire clan to set foot on foreign soil. He left India at eighteen, just after high school, in search of freedom and the bright lights that took his fancy whenever he watched those Hollywood movies. Back then a student visa to New Zealand was easier and cheaper to obtain than one to America or the UK.

I met him at a time in my life when nothing was going right. Love was a far-fetched idea for me. True love that is. I'd had my share of flings, but nothing serious, just a few months on, a few months off. One thing I was a firm believer in was that I would never marry an Indian man. "They all screw around, drink too much, and come home and beat their wives," I used to tell Ma. At least that's what I grew up learning in my parents' home anyway.

Then, just when I had bought a four-hundred-dollar backpack to travel the world and become a hippy, Gurveer came into my life and transformed it into a quicksand of love that sucked me in so deeply I learnt to believe in true love again.

He loved me and proved to me that not all Indian men hit their wives. Hard to believe at first, but with each passing day I realised he was the one, and when he finally popped the M word I hugged him tightly and nodded my acceptance.

It came as a surprise to my family when I told them I was marrying Gurveer and that we would have the wedding in India. I told Ma first, then Pouja, then finally Pappa.

I'm not sure whether it was a bigger deal to them

that Gurveer was not a Gujrati or that I had finally decided to settle down when all hope of my marriage had been lost. According to my parents and certain relatives whom I prefer not to name I was way beyond marriageable age.

"Chee chee, so late. Stupid girl. She doesn't stand much chance of having babies. These girls nowadays don't realise their eggs aren't there forever."

I was twenty-five then. But of course most Gujrati girls get married off at eighteen, twenty-one at the latest. And so they are probably grandmothers in their early forties. Ma had Pouja when she was sixteen and became a grandma at thirty-eight. THIRTY-EIGHT! Salesh, my nephew was born when Pouja was twenty-two, a year before she divorced Salesh's father who like many Indian men, hit her and drank too much. And so marriage at twenty-five made me appear antique to my relatives.

Coupled with a "late marriage" decision, it was my desire to go to India that really took the icing off the cake if there was any icing in the first place, that is. Ma was hysterical, Pouja was "kinda sad to see you go kiddo", Pappa said "Keep your passport with you at all times and don't give more than one rupee exactly to any beggar at any given time," and Daksha Auntie, though one notch less hysterical than Ma, was hysterical nonetheless.

And then there was the big issue about the Sikh faith and their turbans!

"Does he wear a turban?"

"What colour is it?"

"How big is it?"

"Do you have to change your name to Kaur or Preet or Deep?"

"Will they make you cover your head?"

"Will he convert you into a Sikh?"

About the faith conversion I had told them "NO", or rather yelled it at them. As for the turban I let them find out for themselves.

To their relief a turban-less Gurveer, sporting a fashionable short haircut and dressed in a beige Punjabi style tunic and cord pants kurta-pyjama outfit, had greeted them in the quiet Indian restaurant, tucked in one of the streets in Mount Roskill, where I had arranged for their first "groom viewing". Ma had tried persuading me to have Gurveer over for dinner but I wanted a neutral ground for their first meeting. Only I knew what my family was capable of blurting out and they would have certainly had the upper hand in their own house.

In the restaurant Gurveer and I politely told my gawking family that we had found a place to move into. You can imagine the verbal bashings I received from my parents at home that night. Unfortunately for them, but fortunately for me, they couldn't really find anything bad to say about Gurveer and I was adamant about moving in with Gurveer so they had to put up with it whether they liked it or not.

After our lavish three thousand guest-list wedding in India, my moolah-loving father was convinced I would have a ball in Punjab with my new family. My own family liked Papa-ji's subtle sense of humour, Bi-ji's mouth-watering dal-makhni curry, Didi's sumptuous golden-brown puris deep fried in homemade ghee, and Pa-ji's uncensored jokes which he never refrained from sharing once he was a little high on his Godfather Beer. And of course Ma knew how much I adored kids so Rannu and Preetu were an instant hit with my family.

Pappa especially enjoyed the house his daughter was going to live in. I had waited till the wedding was over before I told them I wasn't ready to go back to New Zealand. Surprisingly, they didn't fall out of their skins and took it rather kindly. Pappa complimented us on the design and architecture of the two-storey concrete house which had a large marble plaque mounted on the front entrance gate, the brass encrypted letters on it reading: CHOUDHARY NIWAS - RESIDENCE OF SHRI HARPAL CHOUDHARY.

My father also nodded his admiration at the large mass of land behind the house that was the family dairy farm plot as well as home to our two Bihari servants and their families and forty-seven cows. A long tube-well, kept clean at all times by Ramu and Raju under Bi-ji's fastidious supervision, ensured the vibrancy of the greenery that surrounded the plot.

Ma and Pappa went for their morning strolls in the alley ways of our street, usually returning through the back entrance of Choudhary Niwas from the dairy farm plot. This entrance took them into a spacious patio, our outside-kitchen. Most of the cooking, and the making of lassi, ghee and makkhan (fresh cream), were done here on the earthen stove. The twin gas stove in the inside kitchen was reserved for making tea, or for cooking small meals that didn't require much preparation, like two-minute noodles, which Didi usually made for the children's after-school snack.

For me, life in Choudhary Niwas is near perfect, if not totally perfect. After a rat-race of a life in Auckland I devour my solitude in my new home and cherish every moment I spend with my new family.

If I had a graph to plot my life from childhood to now, the trough on it would reflect my time before marriage. Especially my childhood.

From the outside my family looked perfect or so most Gujrati families who knew us thought. We were the envy of many. My father, Vikas Patel and our Kaka (uncle) Bilas skilfully managed the family garment factory business in Suva, Fiji. Ma and Shanta Kaki (Uncle Bilas's wife) got to wear the finest silks because of the flourishing business. Their saris were often the talk of our street where our two families lived together "happily".

Ma often reminded me that I can't wish for everything to be perfect. Yet I've always felt that my sister Pouja is perfect and that everything perfect always happens to her. She has the perfect waistline which never thickens like mine does even at a sip of water. She also has perfect Hindi-film-heroine's facial features - wide almond Sridevi eyes, Saira Banu's thin, sharp nose and Rekha's pout. Her thick, black hair complements her flawless, milky white skin. And she has a serious eye for fashion.

We look nothing alike. She often reduced me to tears by telling me that I was actually found in a dumpster and wasn't her blood sister.

The saying, "If you tell someone he is stupid he eventually believes it to be true," held true for me about my parentage. Soon I started to believe Pouja when she told me I was adopted. She could have been right because indeed we have nothing in common. I have a big fat nose, no waistline, am much taller than Ma and Pouja, have too much hair on my arms and legs for a girl, and have been told that I talk too much for a girl as well!

Pouja was also the perfect daughter and Daadi Ma's perfect granddaughter, though I have always believed that if our Naani Ma, Ma's mother, was alive I would be her favourite simply because Pouja was Daadi's favourite.

There were so many other things that Pouja and I were dissimilar in. Like colours, for instance. Her fair skin lets her get away with the brightest of colours, her favourite being fuchsia. Mine is blue, though this could be because blue was the first colour I began to recognise as a baby since all my clothes and toys were bought before I was born and they were all blue. Blue, the colour to decorate a boy child with! And just because a dread-locked swami at the Durga temple told my mother that the second child would definitely be a boy.

Coming seven years after my big sister was born, the second child had to be a boy. At any cost. Multiple trips to the temple. Offerings of money, prasadam, red Mata-shingaar shawls. Anything to please the goddess.

Please let this one be a boy, begged my mother. Had her brothers let her continue her education she would have known from her biology classes that it wasn't up to her to decide if Pouja was a girl or I a boy.

Well, what a surprise it must have been to see a determined girl make her way out into the world where the penis rules!

Daadi disliked me the moment news travelled to her that Ma had given birth to another girl. No wonder no one came to visit the new baby at the hospital!

Though I guess what made things particularly difficult for the Patels to accept me was that Ma had had a terrible haemorrhage while delivering me. Later the doctor warned her that bearing another child could put her life in danger. As it was she was always chronically anaemic.

So they were stuck with me. All hopes for a boy baby ruined as I, the unwelcome girl baby, made my way into this world amid a splatter of blood. Utterly unforgivable!

It soon became a habit for me to live in the shadows of the other children in the house. There were four of us. Me and Pouja. And Jaynesh and Sushila, our first cousins - children of Bilas Kaka and Shanta Kaki. Everyone was older than me and knew so much more.

Even when I achieved first place at school or won a debate or oratory contest, Daadi always dismissed it by saying something like, "If only Vikas had a son instead of you he'd be making us proud today with more trophies."

What my six-year-old mind couldn't fathom was how someone could do better than achieving first place in class. Her comments confused me. Though we were taught to address our grandmother as Daadi, father's mother, I secretly referred to her as Cruella when I bitched about her to my school friends Dipika, Jalpa, and Kaajal.

My childhood, as you can imagine, was a series of reminders that I should have been a boy and a series of comparisons that showed I was not good enough like my sister and cousins.

My ultimate weapon of defence was my big mouth. I learnt to laugh at Daadi's insults, Ma's submissiveness to the whole thing, and Pappa's indifference to my existence. Shanta Kaki and Bilas Kaka were always nice to me but then they were nice to everyone. They were the sort of people who would bestow compliments on someone whilst pursing their lips and clenching their teeth and muttering some form of curse under their breaths.

One of the few good things I cherish about my childhood is growing up in a joint family. There was always someone around, albeit in a nagging sort of a way and each evening before dinner Ma and Kaki courteously exchanged a bowl of whatever each one had cooked that day. At least I didn't have to grow up in the dark, smelly dumpster all by myself where Pouja said I was found.

Before I was born when Pouja would have been two maybe three years old, Daada-ji, my grandfather, passed away and Daadi, the family matriarch, moved into the Toorak Road house where her two married sons lived. We all lived together in this two-storey house that had four bedrooms, a bathroom, a toilet and a kitchen on the top floor and then the same thing again downstairs. The upstairs balcony was where we flew our kites from, or wrapped ourselves in our mothers' discarded saris to play housewives, shop-owners, or film stars.

My father, whom Pouja and I have always addressed as Pappa, is the older son. Bilas Kaka was Daadi's favourite, so when Shanta Kaki married Bilas Kaka she automatically became Daadi's favourite daughter-in-law.

Ma didn't mind anything Daadi did or said to constantly insult her because she had failed to give birth to an heir for Pappa's garment factory fortune.

Daadi's favourite grandchild was Jaynesh, then Pouja, and then Sushila. I wasn't even worthy of being the least favourite. As far as Daadi was concerned I was just another burden - an ill-fated child who regrettably had to have money spent on it for food, clothing and an education.

My fondest memories are of my school days. I went to Mahatma Gandhi Memorial School, named after the Mahatma himself. But that wasn't the reason our parents had chosen to send us to this school. The real reason was that this was where most Gujju (as most non-Gujratis preferred to call us) kids were sent by their parents to get a decent education.

We took pride in our school badges which

displayed the acronym MGMS. The kids from rival schools, however, teased us with a slogan of their own version for this: "Moose Ghandaye Master Soonghe", they yelled at us in unison each time our bus went passed their school gates. Literally it meant Mouse Stinks Master Smells.

Still, that is the school I knew and loved, and treated as my sanctuary.

While so many children looked forward to weekends and long school holidays, I dreaded them and used to find as many excuses as possible to stay outdoors. During the term time I'd hang around school as late as possible each day, and consequently became an all-rounder, achieving excellent results in both my class work and extra curricular activities. My big mouth helped me win debates and oratory competitions. A plethora of unconstructive criticisms at home strangely gave me renewed confidence and made me a better performer on stage where I won many dance and drama competitions.

No one judged me at school, or at least no one made me feel bad about the person I was. My singing, dancing, acting, everything became my reason to get up in the morning to catch the earlier bus to school while Pouja, Jaynesh, and Sushila whinged and threw tantrums about mismatching socks or some other dim-witted thing. My teachers and classmates became my real family, showering me with praises and shoulder pats that I never stood a chance of receiving at home.

And then one tragic day when I was eleven years old and in my first year of high school it all came to an end, because Pappa announced that we were moving to New Zealand. I cried all night and refused to eat the dhokla that Ma had made for everyone. I even threw tantrums, hoping to get attention so that these stupid plans were changed and I would once again be allowed to go back to my friends. But nothing like that was ever going to happen.

In fact schools had been temporarily closed though it wasn't the holidays, because on 14the May 1987 a native Fijian soldier - sporting a handsome moustache, which later became a fashion trend amongst native men - had toppled the government and was being hailed as the man behind the first military coup in Fiji. I still remember the curfews that started at 8 p.m. sharp and the streets being barricaded with orange and white rectangular blocks. We didn't have TV in Fiji at the time so all the news came on the radio.

Loots, riots, and temple burnings transformed the "friendliest island destination" of the world into a tourist's nightmare, and the economy plummeted. My family endlessly discussed with visiting relatives the house-arrest situation of the deposed politicians, confusing me with phrases like, "Bloody curly-haired Fijian bastards." Were we not Fijians too?

It made me uncomfortable to remember the hugs and food that my native friend Mereoni and I used to exchange.

"Bula, Prreeya baini," Mereoni would greet me, calling me sister. She'd be sitting outside Fong Yee's Bakery at the end of our street, using the timber slats placed on top of each other as a bench.

"Bula, Mere," I'd reply, handing her a small brown paper bag with dried mango skin that I'd just bought from the Chinese shop next to the bakery.

"Eh, Prreeya, can you give me your roti curry today? Here, you take my dalo cassava and tinned mutton."

And that's how we'd spent many lunchtimes, she eating from my blue lunchbox and sipping raspberry cordial from my blue plastic guitar-shaped juice bottle, and me eating her lunch that had been wrapped in tattered plastic and ragged *Fiji Times* newspaper.

An unknown fear crept inside now as I imagined my parents' reaction if they discovered that I'd been sharing food with a "curly-haired Fijian bastard". Next time, I reminded myself, I'd have to ignore Mere no matter how tasty the palusami in her lovo smelt.

The remainder was pointless, as it turned out. No matter how much I griped nothing was going to change Pappa's plans.

"This country is ruined, we can't bring up our children here any more. It's decided, we're leaving," I heard him tell Ma. "The Australians and New Zealanders have shown sympathy and opened their doors to us suffering Indians. If we don't go now we'll regret it forever. It doesn't look like these arseholes will be able to restore this country's welfare again. They can't even get the constitution right!"

For the next few days each dinnertime conversation revolved around this topic. Pappa was nothing like his father, who'd been a non-violent, humble Gandhi follower and had marched with the Mahatma to gain India's independence. I wondered how Daada-ji would have handled this day if he'd been alive.

Pappa's every word was coated with resentment and hatred. "Their stupid communal land ownership stuff won't work. What about the hard work and sweat that our forefathers put into making this country into what it is today? Some fool with a trendy moustache thinks he knows how to run this place. Bloody fool! I'm telling you, it's not Cakabau's days any more. These idiots don't have any respect for Cakabau's principles just like how our Indians in India have forgotten about

Gandhi's teachings. Bapu wanted peace, but as soon as he died what did they do? Yes, yes, bloody divided the nation and they're still fighting for Kashmir. We simply cannot live here anymore and there's no way we can dream of going back to India."

I had never seen him this furious before. I was still horrified by the thought of leaving everything behind and going to a foreign country but it excited Pouja.

"We leave for Auckland in the next two days," Pappa announced one evening. "Lodhia is doing the tickets for me as we speak. Better to leave before these extortionists do further damage to this country. Bastards, their minds will remain as twisted as their tight curly hair. Their stupid chiefly system, Mataqali theories and kere-kere loan systems will put this country to shame. You watch, this country will become a platform for coups now. Not even five months have passed since the first one and they've done another one. That big-moustache man is a curse to this nation."

Ma had remained quiet, mostly out of habit. She didn't dare interrupt Pappa when he spoke in case a thunderous slap landed on her face as it sometimes did.

When enough time had passed since his last sentence to assure her, she placed one arm around Pouja and the other around me and asked, "What about Ba? Who will take care of her if we leave so soon?" Despite Daadi's injustices Ma always had a soft spot for her. Pouja and I watched Pappa's face. Our heads leaned against Ma's bulging midriff like a Siamese twins.

Pappa had it all figured out. "She'll continue staying here with Bilas. I've already discussed this with him and he says it's fine. It won't be long before he'll get a visa to Canada and then he'll take Shanta Ben, the kids and Ba with him. Besides, Ba would choose to die here rather than live with me!"

"And the factory?" Ma asked. Her eyes carefully examined Pappa's hands to make sure they were a safe distance away from her face.

"We've closed that, we'll think about selling it once Bilas and I are settled overseas. For now don't you worry, that's my problem. All I know is the sooner we get out of this hellhole the better!" He sounded unusually calm.

So the two brothers had secretly made their plans to leave our paradise island nation. Opinions from little people like me were not required - we were merely required to help the big people pack. With clothes sorted, and money and valuables stashed away in secret compartments of the trunk, we left stealthily in a late-night taxi for Nadi airport, like thieves breaking out of a prison.

Life for me transformed into something like the American movies we used to watch in Fiji on the VHS tapes borrowed from Raniga Video World.

Freedom was everywhere in Auckland - at school, in the buses, in the city, in the malls, and gradually at our suburban home in Howick.

It wasn't as difficult to adjust to the Kiwi way of life as I had imagined it to be. Even schoolwork was a lot simpler than what I was used to back in MGMS, and I was the best speller in my class. Though I was kindly reminded many times by the Kiwi teachers not to address them as Sir or Madam - if we had failed to use these terms to address our teachers in Fiji we would have been caned.

Each passing day I became a little less Fijian and a little more Kiwi. Later, at university, I enrolled in a Bachelor of Accounting degree which I never completed. It was a foolish course to choose in the first place. What I really should have applied for was medicine. I was a brilliant science student. But I was quite good at English literature as well and with my big mouth maybe I would have done well in a Mass Communication degree. I hated economics with a passion. So many confusing graphs and models to bring everything to a lousy equilibrium - as if life is ever that!

Halfway through university I eventually figured out that the only exciting thing about AUT anymore was the dance parties put up by the Indian Students Association. Bad reason to keep accumulating student loans. Thus began my search for something that was meaningful to me and the world.

A few years passed. I did a general interest course here and there while working fulltime in a debt collection agency. As school had been before, work became my hideout from my bickering family.

Then one day a short, bespectacled gentleman, a work colleague, very sweetly suggested that I try my hands at natural therapy. Up until that moment I'd never known something of that nature existed.

New-ageism had crept into New Zealand from California and had become quite popular. People who, like me, were too lost to decide what to do with their lives enrolled in a natural therapy course of some sort, seeking some form of spiritual guidance.

The college prospectus I ordered mesmerised me with courses on Energetic Healing, Crystal Healing, Remedial Therapies, Yoga, Holistic Counselling, Aromatherapy, Naturopathy, Homeopathy and then suddenly I saw the magic words. Ayurveda: traditional Indian medicine.

And so I began my two-year part-time Ayurveda Life Consultant course. There was no way that Mr Stingy Vikas Patel was going to pay three and half grand tuition fees for me to do a "Crazy desi medicine course that has no future money prospects". So, I juggled my call centre day job with evening Ayurveda classes and weekend clinical training.

With my time equally divided between my textbooks and a telephone headset broadcasting irate, whinging callers, I hardly spent any time at home. Socialising was out too - the only thing that brushed against my boobs was my course notes folder as I clutched onto it in the train on my way to class. There were no kisses on my lips, just my Parker pen, chewed on vigorously while I thought about which treatments would suit various dosha types. A weekly catch up with Tammy was my only sanity fix.

Although I needed someone to love, it never became a priority. I had seen too much misery with Pouja's failed marriage and Ma and Pappa's constant fights to want to jump into a similar deal, especially with an Indian man.

"Stop being racist," Tammy often scolded me. "I'm sure they're not all the same. Who knows maybe you'll meet someone great, what are you going to do, reject him only because he is Indian? Besides, never say never."

She was so right. Soon after I graduated with my Ayurveda Level IV certificate I planned to take off on a backpacking trip around the world and probably do further Ayurvedic studies in India, depending on my cash flow after the trip. My alternative plan was to remain in India and do volunteer work with destitute people. And then out of the blue my life took a hundred and eighty degree turn.

Daksha Auntie was visiting from Queenstown with her forty-year-old unmarried cousin, Jamna Ben. Their friendship surprised people. How could two women so unlike each other get on like a house on fire? Daksha Auntie - short, stumpy, triple-chinned, her hair always in a tidy bun - was an incessant chatterer while Jamna Ben, lanky, with bushy shoulder-length curly hair, was a woman of few words. My guess was their closeness had a lot to do with their similar love lives - each having always loved a married man who was too clever to abandon his wife and children for greener pastures.

Their visit coincided with my graduation, and yet another one of Pouja's break-ups with a loser boyfriend. We decided to have a we-hate-men night out.

Daring to be a little wild, we picked the Aashiq Indian nightclub, famous for its Bollywood remixes. It had a massive dance floor with half-dressed teeny-bopper girls drooled over by Indian and Pakistani dudes looking to get lucky, both sexually as well as visa wise. These Indian joints were known to be infested with illegal immigrants hoping to hook up with a permanent resident or Kiwi citizen and get a spouse-visa, which they'd be prepared to pay up to twenty thousand dollars for.

It was a September night. Spring was a little hotter than usual, and while the rest of the ladies were boogieing on a Daler Mehendi number I opted for some fresh air. I figured there would hardly be anyone rowdy outside since the floor was packed with sweaty bodies rubbing against each other, some intentionally, others accidentally.

As I gazed at the stars, wondering where my destiny was leading me to, a red Mitsubishi Lancer with blaring music drove past me slowly, the driver and four other male companions eagerly looking for a parking spot. A few minutes later it was reversed perfectly to a stop behind a mag-wheeled, black Mazda sports car.

The thumping Punjabi Bhangra music came to an abrupt silence. The four passengers strode into the club without waiting for their chauffeur. Their driver, a tall, fair young man with a handsome face that had a slight resemblance to Craig David, my hot favourite at the time, adjusted his beige Reebok cap in the flap mirror and stepped out of the car. A press on the car keys in his palm set off four little orange lights in each corner of the metallic red Lancer, a clicking sound confirming the doors were locked. He checked for traffic on both sides as we're taught in school, before striding across the road heading, it seemed, straight towards me. A friendly smile broke on his face, followed by a little nod. I smiled back and whispered a little, "Hi."

He entered the club, and through the glass doors I saw him pay his ten-dollars entry fee, get his wrist stamped, and to my surprise walk back out, this time definitely in my direction.""Um…are you okay?" he asked. "I mean, do you need help with your car or something?"

Did it look like I needed help with my car? I smiled weakly and shook my head. "No, I'm fine, thanks. Just needed a little air. Way too smoky in there."

I was smiling a little too much now, I realised. *He's not your type, Priya, and he's Indian, stop showing your crooked teeth so much!*

He placed one hand in his pocket to bring out his mobile phone.

Oh no, see? He's only just known you for two seconds and now he's going to ask for your number. Quick, make one up.

Then he punched a little button on his mobile keypad I realised he was in fact turning it to vibration mode and hardly about to ask me for my number.

"Wanna come in or do you still need some more air?" he asked, placing the cell phone inside his sleek, black, trendy jacket. His voice was confident and friendly. Extending his right hand, his silver kara bangle shining under the street light, he continued, "Sorry, I forgot to introduce myself. I'm Gurveer Choudhary. And you are?"

"Priyanka Patel, but everyone calls me Priya. Nice to meet you, Gurveer," I took his hand, which gripped mine firmly.

"You go ahead, I'll come a little later. Your friends are probably wondering where you are."

"Nah, nothing like that. They're actually my flatmates. One of them is the birthday boy tonight. I usually don't come to Indian joints. I prefer Western music. These guys like the desi music, plus they all wanted to drink tonight so here I am being a good Samaritan. How about you? You come here often?"

"Not at all. Me too...I'm the designated driver for four other ladies."

"Girlfriends' night out then?"

"Actually it's a bit sad - I'm here with my mum, my aunt, her best friend and my big sister."

Raising his eyebrows and grinning, he said, "Wow, that's great. It's about time people went out clubbing as a family!"

As we continued talking I found I was enjoying his sense of humour. He was genuine, and didn't throw stupid one-liners that most useless Indian blokes were so in famous for.

It wasn't until Pouja came out looking for me that I realised I'd been talking to this Gurveer person for almost forty minutes. Seeing Pouja's tipsy state and unstoppable giggles, I excused myself from my new acquaintance and followed my half-drunk sister back into the dark, smoky club.

Some hours later the DJ announced he was wrapping it up for the night and playing the last song. I was making my way outside, trying to get there before the crowd did, when a tap on my shoulder caused me to look behind.

Gurveer, the mobile phone again in his hand, asked, "Would you mind if I gave you a call sometime to catch up?"

Catch up with what? "Sure," I replied, my eyelids batting a little.

It must have been the politeness and the gentlemanly tone he used, and maybe not having felt any interest in a man in the last four years. I was normally very particular about whom I gave my contact details to, but I found myself reciting all three of my phone numbers - home, work, and mobile.

The next day we were on the phone for an hour. Three days afterwards we met for lunch and a stroll on Mission Bay Beach, where we had our first kiss. Three weeks later he told me he loved me and two months after that we were engaged. Thinking back now, I'm certain I fell in love with him on our first lunch date. Before the first kiss.

Chapter Three

Foreign Correspondence

My favourite part of the day at Choudhary Niwas is dawn. This is probably the one time in my life I haven't needed an alarm clock to wake me up.

Instead, it's the distant sounds of peace coming from three independent holy buildings bhajans from the shiva temple at the end of our street, kirtans from the Gurdwara, and the azaan from the mosque. All three sounds beginning and ending in their own rhythm, blending with each other from time to time without disrupting each others melodies. All three spreading the same message. And yet all three a victim of gruesome discrimination by a handful of Nehru-collared, khadi-clad politicians who have probably never heard the sounds of peace and serenity that my ears are blessed with each morning.

If only they did hear these serene voices, India would be a much better place to live in, and bigger too - no Indo-Pakistan border. No jawans dying everyday at Kashmir LOC, no burning of temples and mosques, and no corrupt goondahs running for elections and coming out winners.

It's six o'clock. I lie awake for a little while longer until Didi commences her daily reminders to Rannu and Preetu to get ready for school. "Nyano, hun tho uth khadho. Tei school nahi jaana aajj..." Didi's koel voice growing stronger in pitch by the passing minute.

Kids get up so early here. It's about time I got up too. My satin pyjamas had me shivering last night. I'll have to wear my flannelette ones from tonight. It seems winter will be colder this year. Summer was hotter than ever - global warming doesn't help.

I peel the covers off me quietly, careful not to wake Gurveer up. He mumbles something in his sleep. Probably a dream, a sweet one, I hope. After slipping my feet into my fleecy slippers I creep to the bathroom. A glint of sunshine appears on the bathroom mirror. I open the curtains, allowing the thin streaks of light to transform into warm beams of golden hues. Damn, Gurveer switched the hot water geyser off last night. The water is going to be ice cold.

I glare at Gurveer, resisting the temptation to throw one of my slippers at his big head for being so careless. After switching the geyser button on, I leave the room to dawdle on the terrace roof. It usually takes a good fifteen minutes at least for the water to heat up.

Didi's scolding has subsided. Rannu and Preetu are in the downstairs bathroom. I can hear them fighting for the wash cloth. Their bodies are used to the "warm" - or so everyone claims - water that comes out of the municipality pipes before seven a.m. Not me. I'm a hot weather, beach person. I love the sun and despise winter. And I especially couldn't have a cold shower. Well, maybe if it was a really stinking hot day the way it gets in Delhi during peak summers then maybe I could. Though even then, I'd have to start the shower hot and gradually move the mixer knob from the red dots to the blue ones.

Wisps of smoke swirl from nearby homes into the morning air. The aroma of skillet-burnt ghee wafts from our outside kitchen. Didi must be making aaloo-gobhi paratha for breakfast from the left-over curry from yesterday. An epitome of a good Punjabi wife, mother and daughter-in-law, Didi never seems to tire of her responsibilities - first the dairy farm, then the kids, and now the kitchen. She's been awake since three a.m. and is still going strong. I wish I could be like her. I wonder if she ever misses not having her own identity, something we Western girls are determined on retaining even after marriage. Like surnames for instance - much to Gurveer's initial qualms I kept my surname. I love you to death but don't you think Priya Patel sounds so much better than Priya Kaur, I had reasoned with him. What I really wanted to declare but didn't, so as not to hurt his already hurt feelings, was, "No way, man, I'm a 21st century woman so don't even try pushing my feminist buttons. It's bad enough that I have to carry my father's lousy family name - don't make it worse!"

The burnt ghee smell makes me feel a bit queasy in the stomach. I walk to the charpoy and sink into it with a thud. Still another few minutes before the geyser will be hot.

In the distance, on a lane that's usually deserted this early in the morning, I notice a crowd of men, women, and children carrying on their shoulders a rectangular box covered with blue silk fabric, walking towards the direction of the Gurdwara which also happens to be in the direction of our house. The men wear navy blue kurta pyjama with turmeric-yellow turbans. Shiny, steel kirpan swords, attached to a black cloth belt worn over one shoulder, hang on the side of their waists. Even the women and some children are wearing one of these symbolic Sikh daggers.

As they approach nearer I realise the procession is a parbhat feri - when Sikhs carry their holy book, *Sri Guru Granth Sahib*, on their shoulders as part of their prayer ritual. A soft chant follows:

"Naanak naam te aa lo ji
Parbhat feri aai hei."

My eyes closed and palms in bowl-shaped prayer position I recite, "Satnaam Wahe Guru" and caress my face immediately afterwards, embracing the blessings of the Ten Sikh Gurus.

The water must be hot by now, I decide. With an unexplained sense of inner happiness I stroll back inside for a clean rub.

*****

I adjust my floral duppatta so it doesn't tangle between my ankles when I go down the stairs and head straight to the puja room to do my morning diya-batti, a lamp-lighting ritual in our home shrine. Gurveer and his family were happy for me to have my own little shrine to observe my Hindu rituals. In fact they've always gone to Hindu temples during important festivals such as Lord Krishna's birthday and Diwali. I give them the same respect by going to the Gurdwara.

Gurveer liked doing diya-batti from when we lived together in Auckland and continued with it in his home which was okay by his parents not that their approval or disapproval meant much to him.

In my little shrine a ceramic idol of Ganesha resides on the centre. Also known as The Elephant God, Ganesha holds a prime position in my life for removing any obstacles that may come. Shiva and his consort, Parvati, sit on the left of Ganesha, while Durga, Lakshmi and Saraswati - goddesses of strength, wealth and knowledge respectively are on his right. Pasted on the wall are colourful, sequin-embellished pictures of Guru Nanak Dev Ji, Baba Balak Nath Ji, Krishna and Shridhi Sai Baba Ji.

I roll some cottonwool into a chick pea sized ball, leaving a small portion of it to twirl into a wick. After dipping the ball into a ghee-filled brass lamp, I chant "Om Shree Ganeshae Namah" three times as I light it. My prayer usually lasts for about fifteen minutes daily, except when I'm "unclean" for seven days once a month. Thankfully now I don't have to worry about that until the baby comes. Then I'll have to follow the six-week abstinence from diya-batti owing to the continuous bleeding.

I conclude my puja rituals, touching my forehead to the ground and thanking Dharti Maa, Mother Earth, for withstanding the burden we selfishly place on her.

There are two more gestures of respect I must perform before I can gulp down my paratha, which Didi will have already laid on the dining table along with my favourite morning read -*The Times Of India (Chandigarh)*.

I'm just in time to catch Papa-ji before he climbs onto his Kinetic scooter to make his rounds in a nearby village, searching for more cattle at bargain prices.

"Peiri peyna, Papa-ji," I say, my duppatta covered head bowed low and my palms touching his black Bata sandals.

"Jinda reh mere pooth," he replies, both his palms placed gently on my head.

One respectful gesture down. Another to go.

Bi-ji, sitting on her charpoy in her room, sees me approaching but pretends she doesn't and begins chanting some mantras on her prayer beads, her way of avoiding a conversation. I touch her feet to do peiri peyna. She chants away with semi closed, quivering eyelids and nods her head in response. No smile. No words. I wonder if her aloofness has to do with our elopement last night.

Didi is halfway through her paratha when I return to the living room for my breakfast. I give her a girly hug. "Morning gorgeous," I say, squeezing her cheek with my thumb and forefinger.

"Morning…go away, not talking to you," she teases.

"But why, my dearest? What have I done?"

She smiles like a mischievous schoolgirl. "So…where did you lovebirds go last night, huh? I told everyone you'd gone out to see some gora friend from New Zealand who was staying at the hotel. Gurveer told me you were going to the doctor…as if! I know you two… Now c'mon, spill the beans. What's up, where'd you go?"

"We needed to get away, Didi. I hope you didn't mind that we didn't invite you and the kids. Next time I promise we will. It's just that it was so great to go out. It's been ages since Gurveer and I did that…are you mad with me?"

"Noooo yaar, of course not. Silly girl, I'm just pulling your leg. I told your Pa-ji you lovey-doveys need your time out. He agrees, actually. In fact he craves for some time out for me and him too."

I swallow a bit of guilt with my paratha. How selfish of me to crave for alone-time with Gurveer when Didi and Pa-ji, married for nearly eight years now, never complain about not having a night out for themselves. Maybe I'll surprise her one of these days to make up for last night. Though I know she never begrudges anything we do.

A woman with a pail calls out for Didi and she has to rush out. We have women coming in the mornings some days to get free lassi. Choudhary Niwas must be the only house where such generosity is possible. With so much milk, why not?

I use my clean "unclean left hand" to flip open the half-folded newspaper. The paper quality is probably half the thickness of the *New Zealand Herald* pages back home but the print quality is good and I have to say the icing on the cake is the sensational words of Indian journalism. I've always believed some of the best writers in the world come from India. Witty, humorous, awe-inspiring.

I glance at the main headline and speed-read the first couple of paragraphs. Thanks to the pyramid rule of journalism one is saved from reading on if the masala stuff of the story gradually turns flat. Not much is new in today's news. Just the same stories with slightly different angles. Page one, something about Jammu-Kashmir. Page two, a little hot and spicy, the usual shit-fight between Badal and Singh, two power hungry politicians who are aiming to make Punjab a better place to live in except they keep letting their egos get in the way.

Next Letters to the Editor, with more public uproar about five witnesses who were too paralysed to intervene when a seventeen-year-old girl was raped in a local Mumbai train. It's exactly one month today since the rape and still none of the witnesses have come forward. How do these people sleep at night? I want to regurgitate my saliva-mixed paratha and spit on these five shameless faces.

The Bollywood gossip on pages four and five lightens my heavy heart a little. A list of hits and flops, and a music masala chart. While the Big B is having a plethora of hits, poor Junior Bachchan is being given the critics' thumbs down. These critics don't even give the poor guy a chance to be his own person. I bet they'll regret it one day when he rises above all the teeny bopper Khan wanna-bes and comes out numero uno. Most fail to realise that he can't be like his father simply because he is a different person. The best part about

Abhishek Bachchan is that he's a balanced mix of Bollywood's top two, Jaya and Amit ji.

The paratha feels sticky between my yoghurt-dipped fingertips. After gulping down the last bite I begin to lick each finger, savouring the lemon pickle tingle. Too much unhappy news is not good for the baby, I finally decide, so I turn to the fashion pages. Lakme India Fashion Week's success is hot topic. Such flowing garments and exquisite accessories. Designers are being sought by celebrities and rich, rich, rich families. My horoscope for today tells me to be aware of conspiring acquaintances, but it also says to look forward to a pleasant change in health. I smile and give my belly a soft pat.

I take a deep breath and lean back on the chair. My mind drifts from the printed news into the reality that surrounds us. These newspapers try and bring to us, as best as they can, everything about India. The underlying reality, however, remains reticent. A reality where a barely-clothed street beggar smiles at you, happy just to be alive today. A reality where a millionaire is frowning at the share prices - Tata down, Birla up, Reliance no-change. A reality where a billionaire is so immune to his own wealth nothing seems to touch him - no hunger, no stock-market slumps, no taxes, no power cuts, no corruption, no ministers, and no underworld bhai-dons. Nothing except counting the thick piles of rokra, as the Gujratis say when they see cash, and of course buying the latest high-tech gadgets.

Then there is the middle-class reality where Gurveer's family fits in. Here, the citizens spend their days working hard to earn extra rupees to give their children a better education whilst battling the epidemic of corruption and dowry that is spreading its cancerous tentacles through every possible part of this country.

I give the paper one last glance and then fold it in half, skipping the sports section except for the fuss about Sachin Tendulkar's duty-free Ferrari. This section's always about cricket or cricketers. Frankly, I get better cricket news from Tara.

Just as I am drying my hands on the red-check tea towel Gurveer walks in. He must have done his puja - I know he won't enter the kitchen until he has done his puja and his peiri peynas.

"You're looking very handsome this morning, daddy-to-be," I whisper in his ears as he hugs me from behind. His sky blue cotton shirt feels crisp against my skin.

"I'm going out with Papa-ji on business," he whispers back.

Squinting my eyes for a brief moment of protest, I click my tongue in irritation. How come he didn't say anything about this earlier? Why am I always the last to know anything in this goddamn house? *Calm down, Priya, calmness is good for your baby.*

As though reading my mind, Gurveer takes my hands into his and kisses my fingers. "Priya, meri jaan, Papa-ji needs me to go with him to Patiala to collect overdue monies. There's a cattle trader who's been dodging his payments for more than six months now. It's a matter of two lakhs. We can't let this guy roam around free any more. Jaan, I meant to tell you earlier but last night was so great, just you and me, the dinner, the drive...I didn't wanna bog you down with all these things."

"I understand, Jaanu," I say, my eyes low. *Do I?* "Will you been gone long?"

"We'll stay the night at someone's house only if it gets too late to drive back. But I'll call you to confirm. Keep the mobile on."

"Love you," I tell him, reassuringly.

"Love you too." He helps himself to the hot paratha and walks out to the porch where Papa-ji is sitting.

It doesn't look like Papa-ji encountered much of a bargain with the cattle earlier otherwise he would be home much later.

He's speaking on the cordless phone in his village dialect, which I haven't been able to fully grasp yet. It sometimes sounds less Punjabi and more Rajasthani - lots of "maaro, thaaro" words. I can't be bothered to learn this one too. As it is, I'm up to my neck in languages, already speaking English, Hindi, Fijian and Gujrati, and now having to learn Punjabi…enough already! It does give me something to boast about every now and then though.

Languages are fascinating to learn. The dialect, tone, flow and pronunciation - each has a way of enlightening you about a person's culture. The French sound romantic, Italians sound passionate, Punjabis sound somewhat patriotic (more towards Punjab than India as a whole), the English sound very proper and correct, while Americans are always optimistic about everything, even terrorism. With Hindi, one couldn't imagine the language being spoken without the head wobbles, and Fijians sound happy and carefree. But when we Gujratis speak, we sound like the twittering of birds coming from trees during twilight - really, really, *really* noisy. My teachers always had us Gujju girls on detention for being the noisiest of the class.

I glance outside every now and then to see if Gurveer has maybe persuaded Papa-ji to change the

Patiala plans. What am I supposed to do all day without him? And how come I'm turning into a possessive lunatic? I never used to be like this. It must be the changes happening in my body. All of a sudden I'm craving attention and sex.

Gurveer and Papa-ji are still discussing something in low voices. I deviate my attention to the TV now that the eavesdropping isn't entertaining any more but I'm interrupted by someone's bicycle bell ringing at the entrance gate.

Didi beats me to the gate and walks back in with a thin stack of envelopes. "He's early today," she says, reading the names on each envelope.

"What's gotten into the mailman this morning? Whose house is on fire that he's in so much of a rush?" I complain.

"Aah, he's just a bit off sometimes. Doesn't help when he has to make these early rounds. Here you go, this one's for you. Looks like Aunty Kavita's handwriting," says Didi, waving a lavender-coloured envelope to me. She has an eye for detail, and has got used to seeing Ma's handwriting on the monthly letters I get. I leap from the velvet burgundy sofa, excited like a little child who is getting her first Diwali money packet.

Ma writes to me religiously. I had asked them not to phone me. It would be too costly with everyone trying to get their two cents' worth into the phone receiver and people here get offended too easily if they are not invited to speak on the phone.

Ma had called me on my birthday last year. She was in Fiji for a week at the time and couldn't talk for long. So after blessing me a hundred or so times and all the I Love You's later I hung up. Fuming, Bi-ji commented, "So, is it something we've done or said that your mother doesn't think me worthy of even a sat sri akaal?" One of my most difficult tasks at Choudhary Niwas is to make sure I stay clear of Bi-ji's easily trodden-on toes.

My index finger dislodges the envelope adhesive. I sniff the inside of the envelope, part of me hoping to inhale the smell of the Pacific Ocean it has crossed. Oh how I miss the ocean. Punjab has lakes and rivers but they are not the same. I miss looking out to the sea with its never-ending distance. I miss the smell of ocean salt, and watching the yachts bobbing in the shimmering Half Moon Bay waters. A memory of the aroma of freshly brewed latte tingles my tongue. Tammy and I often sipped lattes from big, oval ceramic bowls, sitting under the umbrella outside the cafes in Mission Bay, the sound of waves dapping against the shores would caress our moods as we indulged in our Saturday brunches.

The abrupt groans of the enlarged matchbox-like white Suzuki Zen, our family car, jolts me back into the reality of an ocean-less Punjab. Before I can unfold the vanilla-scented, floral paper Gurveer announces he is leaving for Patiala now.

"You wanna read Ma's letter?" I ask, waving the lilac sachet at him.

"We're late already, jaan. Take care." He extends his thumb and little finger into a make-believe phone and places it on his ear, telling me he will call me in the evening. I extend my thumb, index finger and little finger and wave him a universal 'I love you' sign. I learnt it from a work colleague who was hearing-impaired, and taught it to Gurveer a few weeks after we met. It saves us from embarrassing ourselves in public. Punjab public I mean. It didn't matter in Auckland, even when we French-kissed in front of a hundred people. It definitely matters here; we can't even yell "I Love You" to each other, let alone tongue-tango.

Dating is frowned upon, and moving in with someone before marriage is basically saying goodbye to one's inheritance money. A good son or daughter sees their life partner for the first time on their wedding day. A good son or daughter makes love to their life partner for the first time the day after the wedding. And a good son or daughter announces they are expecting a baby six weeks later, at most. An even better son or daughter announces they are having a son.

I fix my eyes on Gurveer as he manoeuvres the steering wheel with his fair, toned hands. Glints of his silver kara dance on the dashboard like minuscule shooting stars. In a few seconds the Zen is far out in the distance, leaving behind a whirl of dust. Time to return to the scented pages from home.

I sometimes wonder if it offends Bi-ji that I never read Ma's letters out loud to her. Though why should I? It's my business what my mother wants to say to me.

I settle myself comfortably on the sofa, placing a mirror-worked cushion on my lap. I turn the TV to mute mode before I begin reading, though there's still too much noise in the periphery - mooing cattle, the distant calls of hawkers, and screaming village children.

Ma writes:

28th August, 2002
Priya Beti,

Hoping this letter finds you in the best of health by the divine grace of Durga Maa. Beti, I haven't heard from you in close to two months now. Is all well with you? How is Beta Gurveer? Give him my aashirvaad. Also give my warmest sat sri akaals to your Ma-in-law, Pa-in-law, Jasveer, Paramjeet, and their adorable kids (Sorry, I forget their names).

Pouja is fine. She too tells me that you haven't been sending her those computer letters. You know, she is now seeing a very nice Kiwi boy - actually he is 48 and a divorcee too. But we're not fussed any more. It's time Pouja settled down once more, with her own choice, if that's what's going to keep the marriage together this time round. Your Pappa still regrets marrying her off to Jitesh Patel... saala kameena duffer is now married to some pakeha girl, I hear. Now I shall see how his mother walks around with her nose bleeding with shame. Bloody kutiya, but no, calling her that would insult the poor female dogs!

Our poor Salesh is not taking things well either. He's only eleven and knows all about divorced parents. My heart breaks to see him one week with Pouja and one week at that arsehole's house, probably being forced to call that white girl "Mummy".

Your Pappa is as usual. Still enjoying his late night society parties. He has been nominated for the presidency for Auckland Patel Samaaj. Beti, I don't care about his womanising anymore. I think the well of tears I once had is now as dry as Jaisalmar dessert. You are lucky to have a loving husband like Gurveer. So what if he is not a Patel, at least he loves you, nah?

Can you believe it's been fifteen years since your Daadi Maa passed away? We had a shraag to mark the anniversary. I missed you a lot that day, Beti. Everyone was asking how you were. You've been gone so long now.

Have you heard back from the immigration folks? How come they are taking so long to give Gurveer his residence visa? Time has changed so much. When we came here getting a visa was easy but now, since the attacks in NYC, it's almost impossible. Poor Beta Gurveer. I suggest you give the immigration people a call and tell them you are a Kiwi citizen. Surely, they must get off their arses and do something to hurry things up!

Oh, I almost forgot to mention...your Aunty Shanta Ben, Uncle Bilas and cousins Jaynesh and Sushila are coming to spend New Year's with us. They'll stay with us for a week and then tour around Australia (that's if the heat there doesn't kill them first!). They said if they like it here they might consider moving here permanently. Toronto is way too cold, they say, and full of way too many Gujratis. But I dare say Auckland is becoming quite the same. I just hope they pick some other city and not Auckland. I couldn't handle living anywhere close to Shanta Ben - too many bad memories.

Now, down to some important matters...

Beti, sorry if I'm going to sound too frank here. Do you realise it's been eleven months since you got married? Isn't there a little Gurveer on the way? Look at Pouja. So what if she got divorced - at least she had Salesh when all her eggs were still intact. How come you haven't got pregnant yet? Is something wrong with your health? Are you getting regular periods? Are your ovaries okay? Are you and Gurveer intimate enough? What, what? Tell me! What are you young women waiting for nowadays? It's crazy. You know, the Kiwi government is trying to pay women to have babies now because young women nowadays are too career minded. Despicable!!!

Think about it, Beti - there's no bigger joy than to hold your own child in your arms. Don't wait too long. Talk to Gurveer. You are twenty seven. Way too old already! Remember, you are in India; if you don't give Gurveer an heir soon his parents might give him non-stop taanà and make his life miserable until he agrees to marry an eighteen year old, same-caste, Punjabi girl who has lots of eggs inside her ready to harvest.

Bake while the oven is still hot, my dearest.

It's almost time for Navratri. Pouja has been getting her ghagra outfits, matching bangles, and other shimmery things ready for each of the nine evenings for daandiya. I'm quite excited too. I've lost some weight so I can fit into my cholis. I'll be sending you the Karva Chauth shagun things by courier soon. Write soon and tell me if there is anything special you'd like from here. Maybe some Western clothes, nah? Farmers is having a big clearance sale and your favourite Sussan shop also has 50% off sale. Pouja is going crazy with her new man's credit card. No scrooge Patel guy would spend like how this boy spends on her. But then he is also getting pleasure from my young Pouja, nah? Only fair.

Beti, I'd better pen off now. Aunty Daksha sends her love. She is not too well. Doctors have put her on insulin injections now! My poor Daksha.

May Durga Maa be with you always.

Big hug and lots of love,

Ma

PS. Could you please send me the genuine DVD of Devdas (not the old one - I want the re-make, with Shahrukh, Aishwarya and Madhuri. Your Pappa got me a fake one from Dubai last month which keeps skipping the Maar Daala song!). And also, please send any latest arti-puja songs.

PSS. Sorry, beti, Pouja wants a nose stud. She says to tell you to send a tiny diamante-type, light pink or purple, to match her Diwali ghaagra outfit.

******

Phew! What a letter! Initially I smile, but gradually my expression turns into a serious frown-like pout. Apart from Salesh, my nephew, I'm hardly enthused by any other details from these aromatic pages. India has shown me such a diversity of circumstances, lives and emotions that Ma's words appear almost irrelevant to the bigger picture of life. They seem out of perspective.

I re-read a few lines and smile, twistedly - not with any sense of joy but anger and frustration. A genuine grin does appear when I read her lecture to "bake while the oven is still hot". Geez, where does she learn expressions like that? And how conveniently she anticipates a "little Gurveer". God forbid that a little Priya should be on the way!

I can only imagine Ma's fuss and Pouja's frivolity when they actually learn that I'm pregnant. I plan to write about it in my reply, which I will do this evening.

But first, a little shopping excursion.

******

"Bhaiya, holi holi chalo," Didi instructs the cycle rickshaw driver to ride slowly. Her expression is one of concern as she lets me have more space to fit my bum on the tiny red vinyl covered seat. She struggles to keep hers from sliding off with each bumpy revolution the cycle tyres make over the rocks and dried dog-poo on the roads.

I remember my first time on one of these cycles. It was like a bad audition for a circus show - I struggled to balance my arse, conceal my bobbing boobs and dodge the gasoline-stench street flies, all at once.

It's not as bad today though. In fact, with Didi's generosity, this is a rather pleasant ride to the Sheesh Mahal Bazaar (Palace of Mirrors Bazaar). I'm yet to find out why it's called this because I haven't seen very many mirrors at all except for the ones the sidewalk barber uses to show his customer what a perfect shave he has performed.

A sweet aroma of jalebi wafts into my nostrils. The cool breeze caresses my cheeks while I embrace the beauty of real Punjab - poverty, pollution, rude drivers, women, men, cattle, naked children waving at us, flashing their never-tiring Colgate smiles, Ganesha statues guarding shopfronts, the smell of sandalwood incense, saris and salwaar-kameezes glittering from showroom windows, and of course more rude drivers but it's still pure magic.

I don't think it matters which part of India one is in, this reality is everywhere. The only thing missing in Punjab to make it my ideal home is - you guessed it - a beach!

"Didi, I've got to buy some DVDs for Ma and a nose stud for Pouja. Can we go to The Gallery first?"

"Sure. Bhaiya, Gallery chalo. Holi, holi," Didi instructs our driver.

I worship books and am besotted by beautiful stationery. I particularly adore journals and cards (blank ones mostly, so I can write how I really feel about the recipient). My favourite hangout in Auckland used to be Queen Street Borders. I would go to the contemporary fiction section or browse in the new age area while Gurveer headed straight for the music section and listened to his bhangra-remixes from Punjabi MC. I particularly found the little boxes of self-help kits really cute: ten-minute pilates, zen meditation, reflexology. The Gallery is a far cry from the bookstores back home; nonetheless, it's the closest I can get to being in my world of books.

With Diwali, the Hindu festival of lights, only a couple more months away, The Gallery has a colourful display of flicker lights, Diwali greeting cards, Ganesha plush toys, sequined and mirror-decorated clay pots bearing fake kalash displays of mango leaves and a coconut top - symbols of the Diwali puja.

"May I help you, ma'am?" asks a kind voice from behind me, as I run my fingers through the DVD titles on the display stand. A gigantic poster of the Bollywood heroine Madhuri Dixit graces the wall above the stand. She sits like an empress, clad in a netted, gold ghagra outfit that must have cost the director of the blockbuster Hindi movie *Devdas*, a tonne of lakhs. Indian designers do not come cheap, especially with the fusion styles emerging on the ramps.

"Ah, yes please," I reply. I turn around to see if Didi is bored since I am taking my jolly old time. On the contrary, she seems quite amused by a plush monkey hanging from the ceiling that whistles each time she walks past it. Someone, somewhere, has created a whistling toy monkey - like there aren't enough whistling perverts on the streets as it is!

The expression on the salesgirl's tired face seems to say, "Will you hurry up, lady? I don't have all day." Her forced smile almost gives away the clenched teeth behind it.

"Yes, sorry. I need a genuine Devdas DVD and some puja ones too. All genuine, please."

She looks at me puzzled. Normally customers would ask for pirated copies to save a few rupees. Only yesterday, I hear, there was a police raid at another music shop after someone complained they'd been sold pirated VCDs. Pirating is big business here since India has no copyright laws. In fact copyright is very conveniently interpreted as the right to copy! Fake music, fake videos, even the bastardisation of classic numbers from Lata, Rafi and Mukesh - all are produced in the good name of remixes. Though people are getting sick of these so-called remixes.

The girl places a sealed *Devdas* DVD on the glass-topped counter in front of me, then begins piling high a plethora of puja, aarti, and mantra CDs and DVDs for me to choose from.

I call over Didi so she can help me pick out the right ones for the Durga devotee who's impatiently waiting for these in Auckland.

"Here, these should be fine," Didi says, handing me three colourful DVDs, one with the Om symbol in gold, another showing Goddess Durga, and the third with a close up of Shiva's face, his third eye glittering with silver paper.

"That will be six hundred rupees, ma'am," says the store owner, clad in his white, starched kurta-pyjama.

"Hi rubba, so much...can't be, please check again," Didi protests in her perfect bargaining tone which I have yet to master.

The shop owner glances at me through the gold-rimmed spectacles resting midway down his nose. He turns to Didi and replies, "Madam here wants genuine stuff, therefore price is more. Fake stuff cheaper. You decide." He hastily brings his attention and gaze back to counting the crisp hundred rupee notes handed to him by another customer eagerly waiting for his turn.

"It's cool, Didi," I whisper into her ears. "It only works out to be around twenty bucks New Zealand. Don't worry really."

"Uff." Didi is not pleased with my giving in so easily. She shrugs and walks to the magazine rack.

I see something else I want so I ask the sales girl to "Wait a moment, please." I hadn't seen an Anne Geddes collection in here before. There is surely a time for everything. I pick up the *AG Baby Journal*. The cover has a little baby dressed up in a bumblebee outfit. It is oh, so cute. Elated with my discovery, I decide I need more magazines to kill time before Gurveer gets home tonight, or maybe tomorrow. Hummm...so many to choose from.

Finally I walk back to the counter with my baby journal and the latest glossy copies of *Filmfare* and *Femina*.

After I've paid a total of eight hundred and ten rupees for the purchases, Didi nearly drags me out of the shop, totally disgusted with my limp efforts to bargain.

"I can't, Didi. It's just too hard to go on battling with them when I know it's not really going to kill my budget."

"Stop thinking like a foreigner. Haven't you heard, when in Rome do as the Romans do? Well, you're an Indian in India, so think like one and fight for all the extra rupees that these mongrels get away with charging you. Toughen up, Priya yaar."

I hate standing around waiting for some snobbish shop owner to agree on a price. I'd rather use that time fruitfully. Yet I know Didi's right - I must learn to bargain like a local. She is a pro at these things. So what if the DVDs were genuine? The stingy shop owner was still making a hefty profit at my expense.

"Well…where to now?" Didi asks.

"Pouja's nose stud," I reply, ticking the items off the shopping list.

"Bhaiya, Sethi Jewellers chalo, holi holi," says Didi. This time the cycle-rickshaw driver is a young boy, probably the same age as Salesh. Something about his eyes reminds me of Salesh's as well. Except there is more inner happiness reflecting from this boy's eyes than my nephew's.

"Will you please let me do the bargaining for the stud? You disappointed me in there. And don't start calculating in dollars in front of them you silly girl. Of course they'll quadruple the price as soon as they realise you are a foreigner," Didi lectures on.

"Yes, all bargaining reins to you, your highness," I reply, giving Didi a japphi, a Punjabi hug.

Didi does all the money dealings in the jewellery shop. I signal to her the design I like and she takes off from my cue. Almost a good forty minutes and high-pitched bargaining tones later, we emerge outside Sethi Jewellers with a sugar crystal sized nose stud for Pouja. Light amethyst-purple, just what she wants.

I'm about to hail another rickshaw for our ride home when Didi is tempted to take a "little look" in Rupali Fashions. I'm not in the mood for saris or salwaar kameezes today. I turn my head from side to side hoping to find an interesting enough shop to kill a few minutes while Didi chats to a salesgirl about the latest Patiala suits, which have extra pleated fabric on the kameez pants and sport a short salwaar top.

A small fluorescent sign catches my eye. I haven't seen this shop before, must be new. Upon reaching closer to it I realise it's an internet café. The board displays the words "Ten rupees for half an hour" in fancy, twirled neon graphics.

I walk in to find mostly young boys crowding around each other, getting excited over some naked white woman's tits flashing on their computer monitors. I pretend not to see them and walk towards the service desk. A young man with a Nike sweater and faded jeans looks up at me through his thin-rimmed glasses resting half way on the sharpest nose I've ever seen. He smiles as soon as he realises I'm a woman and not a pornography-starved, hormonally-haywired teenage boy.

"Ma'am, please come in. We have a terminal in the corner there. Please, please make yourself comfortable," he says apologetically. Glaring at his maniac patrons, he turns to face me and grins broadly. "If any help, let me know, my name is Vicky." He fidgets as he guides me to a secluded desk with a Compac PC.

It's been a few weeks since I last checked my e-mail. I hold my breath slightly as the screen flashes up my inbox, showing that I have "3 unread messages".

31st August   Tammy Carmen
24th August   Radhika Menon
18th August   Pouja Patel

I glide the little arrow over the screen and double-click on Tammy's name. She writes:

Hey girlfriend,

Long time, no mail. Hope you're doing well. Tell Guru I said hi. Hurry up and get back here. I really miss our coffee n cake chats. Email soon, sweetie. Missing you heaps. Work is good. We've just merged with another finance company so I have lots more accounts to handle now. I'm going for my para-planner exam soon. Pray for me. Mum says hi. Are you guys going backpacking like how you planned? Gotta go. Love you heaps. Take care, T

Radhika writes:

Hi Priyanka,

How are you? Thought I'd drop you a line or two. We miss you here at work. Nothing new. Harry's left for the sales rep role. Janine's gone on maternity leave. Oh, and we have a new customer services manager. She's got some balls. We get along really well. Reminds me of you. Everyone misses you. Hope you are enjoying married life. My parents want me to find someone suitable too. I met this Muslim guy on-line. He seems really nice. But you know my folks, they'll kill me if I tell them I like a Muslim boy. Must find a Tamil boy…and soon, because they're threatening to write to my aunty in Chennai. God, the last thing I want is some loin-cloth clad Madrasi boy with his head wobbling yat-pat-yat-pat. I wish I was lucky like you. Write back soon.

Hugs,
Radhika Menon
Senior Customer Services Officer

Pouja writes:

Sis,

What's wrong? How come you haven't emailed for ages? Is everything all right? Ma's freaking out. Anyway, I'm good. I'm seeing a really nice Kiwi guy. His name is Anthony. We're going to the Gold Coast this weekend. He's booked the new Versace Hotel for us for three nights. Ooooh…can't wait. Salesh is good. He really misses you. Send him an email okay? He received some more awards at school. Gotta go back and balance the GST statement now. I hate my job!!!

Write soon. Say hi to Guru.

Love you always,

Pooh.

All nice happy e-mails but I don't have time to reply to any of them just yet. I glance at my wristwatch; twenty minutes have flown by. Didi must be done with her chatting-cum-bargaining-cum-purchasing. I pay this Vicky dude his ten rupees and stride back to Rupali Fashions.

God, Didi is helping herself to the Limca and pakoras a salesgirl is serving her. She must have spent a hefty sum for such an appetizing customer service.

"Don't be silly," Didi mumbles, the spinach getting stuck between her teeth. "I haven't bought anything yet. But of course a customer is God sent, nah? So treat the customer like how you treat God. Simple. Here, have some." She hands me the imli chutney dipped pakora and her half full Limca buddy bottle.

Sounds logical! Besides I'm not going to argue on an empty stomach. I take small, shy bites, glancing here and there for someone to notice our true motives. Salesmen drape themselves with the latest saris copied from TV serials *Kyon Ki Saas Bhi Kabhi Bahu Thi* (Because a Mother-in-law Was a Daughter-in-law Once Too), *Kitty Party*, and *Kumkum* - to lure the women customers. The shop owner is busy counting stapled piles of rupee notes. Half he will bank, half he will keep in his black tijori money safe.

"Changa ji, appa phir kadi le lenge. Changa ji." Didi politely tells the sales girl she will think about her choices and come back later. Only I know the hidden meaning behind the secretive smile she gives me. Free lunch, what more do we want?

Later things are quiet at Choudhary Niwas, with Bi-ji having her midday nap. Didi decides to do the same. The kids aren't back from school yet and Pa-ji is having his usual social congregation with the gamblers. Papa-ji has not spoken to Pa-ji for ten days now. "Not until he pulls up his socks and helps me in the business like Gurveer does. Shame on him, chota pra kaam karda, badda hei ga nikkamma!" Younger brother helps and older one is good for nothing!

I place the Gallery's shopping bag on my bed and change into a casual salwaar kameez.

Hi, you in there, we had a busy day today, didn't we, baby? I caress my belly and massage some almond oil to help give my belly elasticity. Ma has soft ridges of stretchmarks on her belly from having Pouja and me. I hope my skin behaves better than Ma's.

Time to do some letter-writing. It's too quiet to concentrate so I put my favourite *Gregorian - Masters of Chant* CD on at a soothing volume that is high enough to fill my room with serenity and low enough not to wake anyone downstairs. Then I begin my long overdue, well thought out letter:

14th September, 2002
My Dearest Ma,

How are you, darling? It's always nice to hear from you. Sorry about being so lazy for the last couple of months.

I've been meaning to call you but I guess life here is way too enjoyable for me to miss home. You've always told us a daughter's real home is her husband's. I can relate to that now. To be honest, if I never move back to Auckland to live again I'll be quite happy. Oh, but I do miss you , Daksha Aunty, and Tammy so very, very much. As soon as the PCO/STD bloke next door fixes his phone I'll call you. Calling from town is too noisy and nosey and we still haven't got the direct-dial system on our home phone yet!

Gurveer is great. You're right, Ma, he's a lovely guy and loves me a lot. Bi-ji, Papa-ji, Pa-ji, Didi, and Harpreet and Ranveer are doing well too. They all send their hellos. Gurveer sends his special love to you and Daksha Aunty. He's just had his medical assessment done so I suspect we should get a reply from immigration in the next couple of months. It's not entirely the immigration department's fault that it's taking so long. The system here sucks. Too many applications are based on fraudulent information. It make things suspicious for the genuine ones. Some people are marrying their own cousins to get visas. Oh, well, what to do. I'll let you know as soon as he gets it.

Ma, sorry about things with you and Pappa. Doesn't sound like he's improving even after all these years. But don't worry. Worrying will only affect your blood pressure. You do your own thing and try and be happy. Let him be a prick if he wants to! Hey, why don't you start doing some yoga again? I try and do my hatha postures every now and then, you know, the ones we learnt in that twelve week course we did at the community centre.

Say hi to Pouja. Glad she's found someone nice. Didn't Pappa freak out that he isn't a Patel? He wasn't fussed at all when I told him Gurveer was a 'cut sar'.

"What's that?" he asked me.

"A Sikh Sardaar who has cut his hair off," I told him.

All he did was raise his black label glass and say, "No turban then, good for him!"

But you know, Ma, a little part of me kinda wanted him to be fussy about Gurveer being Sikh and not Gujrati. I wanted Pappa to treat me like how he treats Pouja.

Oh well. Letting bygones be just that, now tell me, how come Daksha Auntie's diabetes has worsened? Hasn't she been drinking her karela juice? Gourd is really good for diabetes patients. Tell her to go see an Ayurvedic doctor for a pulse diagnosis. She has to stop eating all the junk and eat a proper diabetic diet that the Ayurvedic doctor will design for her.

One of these days I might send Sushila and Jaynesh an email and ask them to come and visit me. Shanta Kaki always goes to Gujarat, tell her Punjab isn't so far away that she can't come visit me once at least. She doesn't even call - that scrooge woman! I still remember how she always wrapped up one of Sushila's old dolls and gave it to me for my birthday each year. Once a stingy, always a stingy!

I'm sending the things you asked for, and Pouja's nose stud as well. Tell her I could only find this purple one, the others were too big - it would look like a fly was sitting on her nose if she wore any of them.

The DVD is genuine and has an excellent "Making of Devdas" chapter. Did you know Aishwarya's ears were bleeding during the Maar Daala shooting? Apparently she got an infection from the earrings. Soooo talented she is, she doesn't let it show in the movie that she was in so much pain! And guess who's pregnant? Madhuri Dixit!!! She's going to have her baby in Denver, USA, where she now lives with her big-time doctor husband. These top Bollywood heroines know how to play their cards right. Tell Pouja she should come and try her luck in Bollywood. She might even find a producer sugar-daddy. She's good at that sort of thing...only kidding , Ma.

Karva Chauth is on October 26th. Make sure you courier the shagun before that. Since the sales will probably be finished by the time you get this letter, just send me whatever you feel would suit me. Don't send any skirts though - way too many perverts on the streets here. Better to send pants. And if you can, please send a couple of rolled-neck sweaters. Size 12 (get 14 if you're buying from Glassons or Max - their 12 is a little tight on my boobs). Also it's going to be winter here soon so no need for any summery stuff. See if the factory shops have any other winter clothes on clearance. If you need help call Tammy - she'll know what I like.

Gotta go now, Ma. I love you heaps. Give my love to Daksha Aunty. Hope you like the stuff. Write back soon. Tell Pouja to email me some latest pics of you all and her new man. Enjoy the Navratri garbah. And tell Salesh that I miss him and love him very much.

Lots of love always,

Priya

PS. Saved the best for last...I'm four weeks PREGNANT!!!! YAY!!!

PSS. Happy now???

Chapter Four

Medicine Woman

A little red X on the flip-top calendar on my bedside table reminds me of my first ultrasound appointment. Today's scan will tell me exactly how many weeks pregnant I am. From my own calculations I should be around nine weeks. The fluttering butterflies in my stomach intensify as I pull a lilac woollen sweater on over my beige salwaar kameez.

Gurveer has arranged for a taxi to take us to Siddhu Ante-Natal Clinic. He reckons it's no longer safe for me to take the motorbike or the cycle rickshaw. "Too many bumps," he says. As for our family Suzuki Zen, Pa-ji has taken it to Chandigarh to attend a friend's wedding - another bachelor bites the arranged-marriage dust.

The clinic walls appear much more cheerful today than when we came to pick up the blood test results confirming my pregnancy. Pictures of babies are pinned on all side, most with a bright, innocent smile though one toddler looks a bit grumpy, afraid of the vaccination needle the nurse is pointing towards his soft bottom and another appears miserable, the literature below her photo telling the reader about teething discomforts.

Things are beginning to sink in. Parenthood is going to be a challenge for sure. Sleepless nights, everyone keeps saying. But also trying to attain the peace of mind that your child is healthy - not just in the moment, or today or tomorrow, but always and forever.

Death too has begun to take a new definition in my life. I've never been afraid of death before. Well, I lie - I've been scared of the way I'll die. I fear dying of a terminal disease or a terrible accident or murder or witchcraft. But I've never been scared of not being alive. I look forward to life after death, to meeting the angels, or farishtas or even God, if I'm lucky.

But now, with my precious little one growing inside me from a tiny cluster of cells into a new person, a mix of me and Gurveer, I'm beginning to fear death. I want death to only touch me when my child is grown up. When my child no longer needs me for food, milk and guidance. When she's become a grown adult and is able to understand that people must die eventually.

"Sweetie, it's our turn," Gurveer's voice jolts me back into reality. "Are you okay?" He's noticed my dazed look.

"Yeah, sorry. Just a little nervous, I guess."

A pale-blue uniformed nurse smiles and helps me climb onto the patient table. She draws the curtains so I can unfasten the bow on my salwar cords.

"Ready, Mrs Choudhary?" Dr Siddhu's voice is polite but firm.

"Haan ji," I call out. *By the way, doc, it's Ms Patel*, I feel like telling him.

Gurveer holds my hand while the pink-turbaned doctor manoeuvres the ultrasound apparatus, which he tells me is called a transducer, in circular motions on my belly. The cool gel smeared on the rounded front part of the transducer hardens the shaved hair bumps on my legs.

A small tunnel-like image appears on the overhead computer monitor. The white background is scattered with grey-black kidney-bean images - here, there and sometimes everywhere. Technology is amazing. Even more amazing is how these images can make sense to anyone. And then I see it. A little dot pulsing. Dhuk-dhuk-dhuk-dhuk. I can almost hear my little one's heart beat.

"Everything looks fine, ma'am. Seems like a frisky little one, doesn't wanna keep still even for a second."

Gurveer's fingers grip mine tightly, his eyes becoming moist as they remain fixed on the monitor. This is our truly special moment, our first real encounter with our own flesh and blood, almost the size of a rice grain and already so "frisky".

An explosion of excitement overwhelms me. Nothing will go wrong now. I just know it. Call it a mother's intuition. I'm unaware of my held breath until Dr Pink-Turban reminds me to, "Just relax, Mrs Choudhary, nearly done." *It's Ms Pat*..oh forget it.

He finally sets me free to get decent and use the toilet in the next room. I hate how they make you drink tonnes of water before an ultrasound. I've had one before, for my kidneys, and remember pacing the medical centre floors in agony. And when I couldn't hold it any longer I abused the nurse who very politely asked me to "Use the loo but pass out only a little, enough to stop the pain." Do these people know that once you start peeing you really can't stop, especially if you've been holding it for more than an hour?

I'm grateful that Dr Siddhu doesn't take too much of our time meandering with small talk. I dress hastily and rush to the toilet next to the scanning room.

My pee seems to take forever. It hurts as it refuses to come out. I whistle a little. Aah, a yellow fountain shoots out, then slows to a trickle and finally to tiny drops that take a lifetime to cease.

When I finally re-emerge in the scanning room the doctor is penning what looks like a prescription script, in his crab-claw handwriting. Hats off to those who can make heads and tails out of this medical calligraphy. He hands Gurveer the script but faces me, saying, "Okay, take the folic once only in the morning, take the iron with orange juice also once a day. And the calcium, only take that when you've reached twelve weeks. Don't lift heavy stuff, try to get plenty of rest and some light exercise - no jogging, just slow slow walking is fine." He pauses, looks at Gurveer and asks, as though Gurveer is carrying this baby and not me, "Now, any questions?"

"Um, thanks doctor," I say, reminding him I exist. "How many weeks am I pregnant then?"

His surprised expression implies this is a dumb question. Maybe he was expecting something more technical like Why do I have to take folic? so he could click his neck, adjust his turban and wobble out a highly technical response about the risks of spina bifida in infants.

He peers down at me through his thick black rimmed glasses. "It's now eight weeks and two days exactly. Anything else?" Again he switches his eyes back to Gurveer.

I glance at Gurveer and raise my eyebrows in case he needs to ask something. Something cleverer than my question.

Gurveer shakes his head. He extends his right hand to shake the doctor's and thank him. "Changa ji, Sat Sri Akaal, Daaktar Saab."

Later that afternoon Gurveer rests his head on my lap while he marvels at the ultrasound photo of our little one. It's hard to make out any body parts yet but it has enough impact to make us behave like two children who have been rewarded with lots and lots of forbidden barfi, the milky sweetmeat.

He yawns and places my palms on his eyes, something he says helps him relax. Drinking lassi with his lunch always makes Gurveer lazy afterwards. The masala dosa was nice at Rummi Da Dhaba roadside eatery but sometimes their servings can go overboard with all the rich spices and yoghurt. I'd read about the indigestion that comes during the first trimester and now it's time to experience its joys. There's always a bitter-sour-curry-spicy-milky stuff that lingers up my food pipe soon after my meals, and a packet of spearmint Tic Tac permanently occupies a space in my handbag.

"Shall we tell them, then?" Gurveer mumbles, relaxed now he knows our baby is healthy and growing well.

It's as if he's read my mind. I've been feeling awkward and guilty for not sharing such wonderful news with Bi-ji and Papa-ji. It's foolish to think that Bi-ji would think of harming my baby if it's a girl. After all, their firstborn was a girl. Besides we do not even know the sex of the baby yet and I don't intend to find out. I'd rather let it be a surprise.

I run my fingers through Gurveer's hair and nod my approval. "Yes, I think we should."

We decide we will tell them this evening. Gurveer leaves for Mintu's garage to find Pa-ji and let him know. I'm in no mood yet to go back downstairs so I pull out the Anne Geddes baby journal from my handbag and prepare to capture my first thoughts about my bub.

I uncap the black felt-tip pen, ready to write down the words that have been bubbling to come out, but then stop. It's not as easy as I thought it would be. I close my eyes to gather my thoughts and create the perfect sentence to document my experiences. No, still no inspiration. Uff, something so simple yet so difficult! It isn't like I'm writing one of my high school oratory speeches, which kept me awake many nights. All of them worth the panda eyes I woke up with each morning, because I won every single contest and was eventually banned from taking part in any other speech contest. Oh, how I cried that afternoon.

"You can coach other students to speak like you," my four-foot-nine-inch, sari-clad principal had told me as she looked up at my five-foot five inches figure.

When I think back now, I am what I am because of my teachers. We had the best teachers, so polite and giving. Sometimes they were American peace corp volunteers coming on a one or two year assignment. I had my first crush on our American maths teacher.

The Ministry of Education sent volunteers only to poor schools, though I'd never thought of my school as poor. We had everything: a nice library albeit with old edition of the *Encyclopaedia Britannica*, a science lab, and a soccer field where native Fijian boys kicked soccer balls without worrying about their flapping sulu skirts showing off toned, mocha thighs. The Indian boys always wore shorts. If only they'd worn the sulu skirts and spoken Fijian the way the natives spoke a pidgin version of our Hindi. And if only we Indian girls with our proper manners and parcelled roti-curry lunches had joined the native girls in a game of netball.

"No, no, we can't play with them, it's not right. We are Indians, superior," some girl would whisper.

Big mistake!

Our parents didn't help either. Always casting a spell of segregation between the two races.

I lie on my bed battling with old memories when I should be weaving new dreams and penning words of optimism in this yellow bumble-bee journal so my baby can read it one day.

And then it comes to me. Of course, silly me, why didn't I think of it earlier? I'm going to write about me - my life, my history - so that my baby will know where Mummy comes from. I will fill the light-yellow pages with my secrets, realities, dreams, and love. I will tell my baby how Mummy and Papa met. I will tell my baby about the scan today.

My writer's block lifts its ugly veil and I begin my perfect introduction:

Friday, 4th October, 2002

> *Hello you, My Tummy Bubba,*
> *This is me, your Mummy-ji.*
> *It is exactly eight weeks and two days today since Lord Ganesha decided to place you in my belly. And already I love you the most in this whole wide universe.*
> *Today, awaiting the day when you are finally in my arms, I make you a promise to take care of you as you grow big and strong in my tummy. I promise to love you unconditionally, now and forever.*
> *This, my sweetheart, is my first gift to you - this journal. In this I will write all the things I want only you to know. Our secret: Mummy and Tummy Bubba's secret.*
> *I love you...forever.*
> *Love, Mumma*

*****

Rannu and Preetu arrive home early today. Their teacher is quite lenient during these festive months. Soon they'll be on their four-day Diwali holiday.

Downstairs Didi is counting out ten crisp one-rupee notes to hand to the vegetable vendor. It is gaajar-muttar-aaloo for dinner today - a carrots-peas-potato curry. The vendor flashes his crooked teeth between his betel stained lips and hands back some free coriander and red chillies. Such fresh organic produce for what converts to a mere eighty cents. The same thing back home would normally cost me eight dollars even if the season was on my side.

Didi spreads out her voile duppatta on the charpouy outside and spreads the peas and carrots on it. She takes the sharp kitchen knife and begins podding and scraping and chopping them, their saffron and green combination akin to the country's flag. I help out dicing the onions and peeling the potatoes, and soon her curry-expert hands have the dinner ready in no time.

"When's Bi-ji and Papa-ji back?" I ask Didi, slurping the last of my lassi.

"Your Pa-ji has gone to pick them up. These weddings are driving me nuts. Now I have to think of what to wear for that Sharma wedding next week."

"Uff, yaar, don't ask me to go too, puhleeese. I can't be bothered. I'll go only if it's a lavish marriage palace kind like ours was - no backyard tent type with all the loud bhangra dhol dhooms," I say, imitating Didi's thick Punjabi accent.

October brings with it two seasons - monsoons and weddings. Papa-ji sometimes gets invited to three weddings on the same day. Not being the type to turn down an invitation, he shows up at every single one with an elegantly wrapped red packet containing one hundred and one rupees for the married couple's shagun.

Cash gifts, whether made to people or bestowed to the temple idols, must be in odd numbers: eleven, twenty-one, fifty-one, one hundred and one, one thousand and one, and so on. Odd numbers bring good fortune - or so say the...well, I'm not sure exactly who says it but I don't argue such beliefs. I was a walking, talking rupee factory on my wedding day.

Choudhary relatives from as far as Rajasthan came to see the "white girl Gurveer brought back from phoren". Unusually, my face wasn't hidden under the netted veil. What a disappointment it must have been to see a bride who was as brown as most of them, and maybe browner than some. My latte skin, that Tammy and my other freckled Kiwi girlfriends were so jealous of, was a subject of much scrutiny in Himani's Beauty Parlour. The three-month pre-bridal skincare package included a "fairness face pack" that I had to apply daily on my face and neck to become the ice maiden that every bride must aim to be. Pity the face pack failed to live up to all the "white girl" promises.

Although my family had wanted on a New Zealand wedding I was all for the three-thousand-guest wedding held in a marriage palace with lots of bhangra dancing. I was besotted with the Punjabi culture and wanted an authentic Punjabi grand event. And there was no way I could have ever had that sort of majesty in Auckland.

It was my day, after all, and I knew my family could come to India, happily flashing their navy passports, but Gurveer's family couldn't come to New Zealand. Not that money was a problem - quite the contrary actually with these Choudharys.

The problem was that no one in Gurveer's family has a passport because there has never been a need for one. And even if they did have passports, getting visas for New Zealand would be a nerve wrecking process. Besides, being part of an ostentatious Punjabi family, there was no way my in-laws would have let their youngest son have a quiet wedding without the colourful tents, umpteen varieties of curries and sweets, loud bhangra music and of course a guest list of three thousand or more Punjabis. Nope, no way at all. And yet in white man's land such a wedding wouldn't be feasible. So the wedding had to be in Punjab and that was final. Despite the would be daughter-in-law being a non-Indian non-Sikh!

Gurveer is always thankful I didn't make a fuss about the wedding not being held in New Zealand, though he would have been happy to get married back home if I had asked him to. But I wanted to experience India and its cultures. Being a Fiji born Indian wasn't the same thing. Deep down I'd always yearned to see India, to be surrounded by my own people, my own culture, my own roots. Don't get me wrong, Fiji is home too, but somehow there was always a peripheral reminder that India was where our real home was.

Now my Indian culture that I so yearned to be a part of has shocked me as many times as it has welcomed me. I grew up listening to stories about India. About how my forefathers were lured to board the ship from India and come to a "paradise" island. About how the paradise quickly turned into hell when they were made to work in the sugarcane plantations by the British rulers. About how when the indentured labour agreements expired some went back to their homeland and some decided to make Fiji their new home. About how they continued to cook their curries, pray to their idols, and speak their varied languages - Hindi, Gujrati, Tamil, Bengali, Urdu and Punjabi, which all eventually transformed into a unique dialect similar to Bhojpuri that is spoken in Bihar and Uttar Pradesh.

And then there were stories about how they kept a safe distance from the natives and sent their children to a separate school. About how India became a memory of a biological mother and Fiji became a reality of a surrogate one.

*****

"Badhaiyaa mere pooth, badhaiyaa," Bi-ji sings her congratulations, hugging Gurveer tightly.

Papa-ji twists both sides of his grey whiskers, smiles, and slaps Gurveer's shoulders with three loud thumps, silently praising his son's manhood.

For a moment they seem to forget all about me. I'm the one who's carrying your grandchild, damn it! I purse my lips into a somewhat fake smile which causes my jaw to hurt. Eventually my turn comes to receive the juffys and puppys - hugs and kisses - from Bi-ji, while Papa-ji places his strong, flat palm on my head and blesses me to give birth to a healthy son.

Aha! What about a healthy daughter, I feel like asking. But of course I know better than to spoil their joyous occasion by wishing such an ill fate.

Gurveer appears a lot more at ease now that the weight of not-telling has lifted off his chest. I can't help but blame myself for having done this to him. Look how happy his parents are. How silly of me to think Bi-ji would say or do anything to hurt my baby. Our baby. Papa-ji's comment about a "healthy son" is a typical chauvinist one and I shouldn't take it to mean anything.

Later, in bed, Gurveer snores softly, his face resting in the crook of my neck. I lie awake watching the dim, silvery light coming in from the street lamps outside. A distant howling dog keeps me company while the rest of the household sleeps, content with the wonderful news of a new life joining them in approximately seven months' time.

Like a wheel of karma my mind weaves countless thoughts - some good, some bad, each new thought giving birth to another, a never-ending process of birth and rebirth.

Ramu's voice shouting his three a.m. wake up calls to Didi and Bi-ji jolts me into realising that I've been awake all night. Not good for my little one - I must sleep. Gurveer turns to face the opposite side. I slide my arm under his and pull my chest close to his back, then press my eyelids together even though sleep seems like an impossible mission.

My eyelids open and close, eventually meeting, heavy with drowsiness.

The amber grills of our room heater makes me yawn every few seconds. Or maybe it's the lack of sleep from last night. Gurveer has gone to someone's wedding with Papa-ji - again! Bi-ji's usual gossip crowd is downstairs and Didi is supervising Ramu and Raju on the dairy farm.

Not one for gossip about daughters-in-law and mothers-in-law, I resort to enjoying my much treasured solitude. My alone-time with me. And of course my bumble bee baby journal. I try thinking of things to write in it today, resorting to childhood memories and those of my time in Auckland. I flip through the family album I brought along with me from New Zealand. There are a few of my baby photos and then some from school, both in Fiji and Auckland.

There's only one of Ma and Pappa, taken on one of their wedding anniversaries. Ma wore an orange sari, chiffon with sequins all over. Pappa had a light blue safari suit on and Pouja, who was about sixteen then, had a pink dress that Daksha Aunty had brought back from her trip to America.

I'm not in the photo as I had insisted on being the photographer for the evening. The new camera, also a present from Daksha Aunty's US trip, gave me a whole new hobby. It also meant I could get away from being mocked for looking dark and chubby in every photo. The next page - the final one in the album - has me and Pouja sitting on the steps outside Aotea Centre. It was taken on my last weekend in Auckland before coming to India.

Pouja had decided to spend the whole day with me at the markets there and buy me a wedding present and little trinkets to remind me of home. We ate Ali Baba's kebabs, drank diet Coke from shiny cans, and licked off each other's ice-creams - hers mango and mine coffee mocha. Strolling from one stall to another we admired vibrant artwork from aspiring artists. We bought each other glass-beaded necklaces. I got her a laughing buddha for good luck. She bought me a phoenix and a dragon. "They bring marital bliss, according to feng shui experts." She also bought me an All Blacks cap, a merino wool scarf, and some kiwi-fruit chocolates wrapped in green and gold packaging.

The photo is so clear I can almost hear Pouja's voice. "You're brave, girl," she had said.

"How so?" I asked, and raised my eyebrows.

"It takes a lot of guts to imigrate to a country you got no idea about. Plus wanting to live with a whole new set of people, people you've only ever spoken on the phone to for what, barely five seconds at a time? Are you scared, kiddo?"

I chewed on the crunchy waffle cone. "Mmm, not really. It's all going to be new for me but I think I'll be fine."

Pouja squinted her eyes, unconvinced. "What if they're really mean to you and make you get on all fours and scrub the floors, and make rotis that pile up to the ceiling?" She groaned at her own words and poked me.

"Nuh-uh...no way, won't work with me. I'm no Cinderella." I nudged her back. "Besides, they all sound really nice. Especially Gurveer's mum, she's a darling. She told me she was forever grateful that I'm bringing her son back to her. She'd lost hope on him going back to India."

Pouja nodded, this time with a serious expression. "At least your Prince Charming is pretty cool. He should be happy you're prepared to move continents for him."

I was silent for a few seconds, thinking about what she had just said. I swallowed the last bit of my cone and wiped my mouth with a tissue. Then I turned to her and said boldly, "I'm not doing it for him. I'm doing it for me."

At first she gave me a yeah-right look, then when she saw I wasn't budging she grew serious. "And why would you do a silly thing like that, kiddo?"

I opened my mouth and closed it again.

Because I want to feel loved. Because Gurveer's family will love me more than my own family ever has. Because I'm sick of Ma and Pappa fighting all the time. Because I'm fed up with you neglecting Salesh for the stupid men in your life, and your constant bickering about how they treat you like shit and how you still "love" them so much. Because I want to be far far away from you all...

I was tempted to say a million things to her, but I didn't want to spoil the perfect day we were having. It was rare for Pouja and I to spend quality time together and today was too good to ruin. I gave her a big squishy hug and whispered, "Let's just call it soul-searching, shall we?"

"I'll miss you, man." She had dark goggles on but I could hear the quiver in her voice.

"Love you, jiji." I rarely called her that. I knew she loved it when I called her "sister" in Hindi so I used it sparingly.

*****

I put away the album and wipe my moist cheeks on my pillowcase. I open my handbag and pull out the bumble-bee journal.

Today I write about my childhood. About my favourite things. My favourite colour.

Blue, of course, since everything I had was blue - toys, clothes, rattle, knitted blankets and shoes too. Ma went on a shopping spree after what the sadhu told her.

"Why blue?" I asked her in my four-year old voice when she related the temple-sadhu episode to me.

"It's the colour of a boy," she explained.

"But I'm a girl," I protested, confused. At the time I couldn't see what the big deal was about being a boy or girl.

"Yes, but you were supposed to be a boy. The gods told me. But, beti, it's bad karma, both yours and mine. Something must have gone wrong at the very last moment." She continued to explain, her words slicing my tiny heart into small bits.

"But what about Pouja? She's a girl, huh!" I asked defensively.

"Her karma's fine. She brought us Lakshmi," was all she replied.

Silly me, faulty me. I finally found a tongue in my mouth and asked, "Ma, what is the colour of a girl?"

She smiled her Promise Clove toothpaste smile and said, "Pink, beti. The colour of girls is pink."

I've hated pink since. But the worst thing is, Ma doesn't think I remember this conversation.

All this I write in the yellow journal, careful not to sound too hateful. I struggle today with a perfect closing paragraph to finish the day's labour. After re-reading what I've written so far, I write:

.........My sweet, sweet child. Grow big, strong and healthy. That is all I want from this universe. I ask for strength to teach you good over evil, love over hate, equality over discrimination, and humanity over cruelty. If you are a girl, I pray for strength for you to remember your identity, your virtues and values, and to live your life to the fullest. If you are boy, I pray for strength for you to remember your identity, your virtues and values, and to live your life to the fullest. It does not matter to me what form you have chosen, girl or boy, for I will love you unconditionally for who you are.

Love,

Mumma

I stare at my last paragraph for a few seconds, taking a long sigh of satisfaction, as though I've finally made it clear to the universe that no one had better mess with me about the gender of my baby like the way they did with Ma.

I'm about to put my journal back in my handbag when a squeaky sound from the chrome door knob turning makes me hide the journal under my lilac pillow instead.

"Pooth, how you feeling?" Bi-ji's sudden appearance is a somewhat pleasant surprise. So kind of her to check up on me, climbing all those cold cement stairs despite her arthritic knees cracking with each step like the sound of gravel underfoot.

Bi-ji rests her palms flat on the mattress and climbs on it, one slow leg at a time. "Shukriya, mere pooth," she thanks me.

With long elongating movements I learnt from the natural therapy college in Auckland, I stroke Bi-ji's thick, fair ankles. The oil seeps into the deep cracks of her heels like water gushing down a river catchment. I make a mental note to get her some 'krak-kreem' I recently saw singing its annoying jingle on TV. The marketing companies must make these jingles irritating on purpose so the viewers will remember their product.

Bi-ji sighs each time I apply a little pressure on the reflex points on her feet. Despite my enormous interest in reflexology I never learnt the meanings of these reflex points. If only Mr Lee was here from the college to interpret Bi-ji's sighs. That's the kidney or the bladder or the liver, he would tell me. For now I have to rely on the warmth of my fingertips and the goodness of my intentions to heal the age-old feet of my mother-in-law.

"Pooth, I wanted to talk to you about something," Bi-ji says, her tone only a little louder than a whisper. She is about to continue when the door is flung open. Tara's strides come to an apologetic halt when she finds the room occupied. Normally she never enters our rooms without knocking first, but seeing the door ajar she probably thought it was safe to come in.

"Haa dasso, ki chaahiye da teinu?" snaps Bi-ji, demanding from Tara an explanation of her brazen entry into my room outside her work hours. The kind expression Bi-ji had minutes ago is replaced by a bigoted frown. She rapidly moves her eyes at Tara, staring at her from head to toe as though ready to leap at her like a hungry lioness.

I have kept to every word of equality I uttered to Tara on my first day as a new bride in this house, so it makes me uneasy to hear Bi-ji address her in this fashion. I decide to intervene, after all, this is my room, my territory, and Tara is most welcome to come in - probably more so than Bi-ji is. "Yes, Tara? Do you need me to help you with something?" I ask.

Tara forces a smile, grateful perhaps that I have retained my parity even in front of her Big Memsahib. "Sorry, Memsahib. I thought maybe I could come for my tuition now and leave early today. There is nothing else to do - everything I've finished doing. But if you busy then no problem. I come back later." Tara glances fearfully at Bi-ji, her eyelids low as she speaks.

"Tuition wooishion, uff. Don't bother us now. You can't see with your own two eyes we are busy? Go wash your eyes, maybe all the dust from the broom has made them weak. Now go. Come later. Better still, don't bother about these tuition wooishion anymore, okay! Choti Bahu needs to rest." Bi-ji holds her fat fingers up in a dismissive manner. She hasn't once looked my way for what I have to say in all this.

"It's okay, Bi-ji," I say, my tone calm like a storm in waiting.

"What okay? Pooth, you need to rest. Too much thinking not good for you, and these servants..." She deliberately trails off mid sentence.

The servants are not to know of such intimate details, as she told Gurveer last night, referring to our pregnancy. Little does she or anyone else in Choudhary Niwas knows that Tara was the first person I told.

"Really, Bi-ji, it's okay," I say. On my bedside table lies a notepad in which I've neatly written some words in large, bold prints. I want Tara to learn their spellings and find their meanings in the dictionary. I stretch my thin hand and pick up the notepad and a mini *Oxford English Dictionary* and *Thesaurus*. Handing them all to Tara, I quickly explain today's syllabus to her.

She smiles her genuine smile this time and eagerly grabs the books from me, clutching them into her chest

like Rannu does with his Nintendo Game N Watch toy.
Then she leaves the room quietly, closing the door
behind her.

Bi-ji's pursed pout changes into a smile. "Pooth,
don't mind but I think you are being too generous with
these servants. They must always be reminded that
shoes can never take the place of a hat. Chalo, not your
fault...you phoren people don't know how deceitful and
cheating these choodhas and chamaars can be."
Choodas, chamaars, achooth - stool caste, shit cleaners,
untouchables.

Born in a congress supporting family with staunch
Gandhians, it makes my blood boil to witness such
cruelty bestowed upon humans who are everything like
us even if the system in this country categorises them in
the lowest possible rank. Gandhi spent many years
trying to enlighten people about humanity, non-
violence, and unity - to eradicate the cancerous caste
system and the harsh treatments of lower caste Indians
by higher caste Brahmins. Harijan, child of god, a term
so aptly coined by the Mahatma himself some six
decades ago, is now blown away into oblivion.

I keep my gaze low so Bi-ji doesn't glimpse my
suppressed rage. I wonder why she is here. It can't be
just to get an aromatherapy foot massage from her
phoren bahu. Hoping to change the thick discomfort that
hangs in the air, I ask, "Bi-ji, you wanted to talk to me
about something. Is everything okay?"

"Aah, yes, pooth. Meri pyaari Priya pooth." My
darling daughter Priya. She takes my oily hands into
her dry cactus-prickly ones. "I've found a really good
medicine woman for you," she whispers, looking around
in case another stool caste might appear from
somewhere.

Genuinely touched by her concern, I reply, "Oh, Bi-ji, I'm already taking some really good supplements to give me energy and make the baby strong and healthy." At least she is concerned, I tell myself.

"No-no-no, pooth, you don't understand," Bi-ji babbles. "But it's okay, it's my mistake. I'll explain. This Medicine Woman will give you a special formula to take. It's only milk, so no need to worry about medicine-type tasting tonic. I met her this morning at satsang and told her you are eight weeks pregnant, like you said last night. She said the timing is perfect. We still have time."

My brain is trying to make sense of her explanation. Is she concerned about my calcium intake? "Bi-ji, the doctor's given me calcium supplements, but he said not to start taking that until I'm twelve weeks pregnant. It's too early to take them at eight weeks, he said."

I hope I'm making sense to her. Sometimes it's hard for me to understand Punjabi - not only the language, but the implications of certain words too. One Punjabi word can have several meanings so one has to be careful about how one pronounces it or the context one uses it in. One can be most embarrassed if one speaks a word that was meant to sound polite but instead sounds crude.

It happened to me when I first came to Choudhary Niwas. Each time I said the word stove - choollah - Gurveer's teenage girl cousins and the older, village women would laugh out so loud I felt like thumping their heads with the wooden rolling pin that Didi used to roll round chapattis with.

It must have been the way I was saying it because later Didi explained that choollah was often crudely used to describe a woman's vagina. "Arre, your hole, yaar!" she smirked.

I wonder if Bi-ji and I are having the same double meaning problem today.

"Uff, pooth, you really not understanding me," continues Bi-ji, agitation in her voice. She probably wishes she had a proper Punjabi daughter-in-law instead of a phoren firengi bahu like me. She puts on a firm tone, still polite but more serious sounding. "Now listen very carefully, pooth. It's not always the Medicine Woman finds the right formula. She told me this time the formula is very good and will work for sure. You just have to drink a small glass of it at four o'clock every morning for seven mornings. I'm sure, with the grace of Wahe Guru, the change - if there is a need for it, that is - will happen. If no need, then all the better."

What the hell is this crazy woman talking about? Milk formula, change? Is she for real? Priya, now is not the time to be a goody goody bahu, I scold myself. I decide to shed the coat of politeness and speak freely. "Bi-ji, what are you talking about? What change? What milk and what goddamn formula? And what is this nonsense about a Medicine Woman?"

Bi-ji jerks her knees to her chest, startled by my anger and directness. "Arre, pooth, calm down. Loud talking is not good for the baby. No need for such bad mood. I'm only advising you to try the milk. If Wahe Guru's blessing is on us I'm sure the formula will change the baby, like I said - but only if there is a need to though."

"Change to what - an animal?" I ask, my tone losing its rationality.

This isn't good. She didn't just come up here with her sack of rattling bones to see if I was feeling all right. Some witch of a mother-in-law she is to walk in here and talk about a stupid Medicine Woman who will change my baby.

"Change my baby to what, Bi-ji?" I repeat, trying hard to be calm. Some cat or dog maybe? Or an addition to the herd of forty-seven cows she already owns?

"To a boy, silly," says Bi-ji, her smile hopeful, as though she has finally made her phoren bahu see the sense in her wise suggestion.

"WHAT? Hang on a second…WHAT did you just say?" I want to say more but the words are refusing to come out. This is all too confusing. The curtains are flapping too loudly from the monsoon winds. My insides are churning like the dark clouds that are rapidly passing over the sun, allowing only patches of sunlight through their grey thickness.

This can't be happening. She didn't say these horrible words. This is not my mother-in-law, this is a sick, sick, sick woman with her sick, sick, sick fantasies. How could she? *Bitch, bitch, you filthy bitch*, I want to yell out at her. *Whoever you are get out of Bi-ji's body and identify yourself you mean spirited being!*

"What the hell did you just say?" I finally manage to scream out.

"Priya!" Bi-ji raises her voice and wags her pointer finger vertically at me. "Keep your voice down. Have some respect for me. Here I am thinking about your welfare but look how you're repaying me, with all these anaap-shanaap obscenities. Dumb girl, what better joy for any woman than to have a son for your first born? Later, maybe try for girl, but only if you want. But we have Harpreet already, nah? No need for another girl. Only seven mornings of this milk and you see the difference a boy will make…."

"Get out." I can't let her finish the evil thoughts she's so effortlessly voicing. "Just. Get. Out. Now. Please, Bi-ji, before I say any more, just leave. Please." I join my palms together, desperately wishing for the earth below to swallow me.

"Pooth, why are you so upset?" Bi-ji asks, surprised.

Does she need me to explain? Very well, stay and hear me out then, you wicked witch.

"Bi-ji, I can't believe you would stoop this low! I'm ashamed of you and your malicious plans for our baby. You of all people, Bi-ji! You are a woman, your first born was a girl and yet you're telling me to drink some crazy formula so I can have a son. Bi-ji, are you out of your freaking mind?"

So engrossed I am in putting my mother-in-law in her place that I don't see Gurveer dash through the doors, obviously shocked at my blaring rage. I've always wondered why Indian men are accused of being mommy's boys, but today I catch a glimpse of the answer.

"Priya, what the hell is going on here? I can hear you from outside the gate. Lower your voice, for God's sake, and tell me what this is all about," demands Gurveer .

"Ask her what the hell is going on, not me. Why are you asking me? She's the one," I retaliate, pointing boldly at Bi-ji. I've had enough and I can't care less about my goody goody phoren bahu image anymore.

"Priyanka, mind your language. Don't cross your boundaries. She's my mother." He's never said my full name in that manner before.

A victorious-cum-sarcastic smirk appears on Bi-ji's face; she is evidently enjoying the much-anticipated display of her son's macho hood. Put *her* in her place, the semi-stretched, pursed lips seem to imply.

I feel like I've swallowed a hand grenade and it's exploding in my stomach. My poor little one, having to listen to all these words of bitterness. *I'm sorry, my sweet, sweet tummy bubba. Forgive me, my darling.* Glaring at Gurveer for his unfairness to his wife and child, I yell, "What do you mean, don't cross the boundaries? Who the fuck do you think I am? I'm your wife, not some bloody servant who must remember their boundaries. Why don't you ask your dearest mother here what malice she carries in her sick mind for our baby?"

Gurveer takes a step back, astounded by my rage. He has only ever seen me like this once before - a week or two before we left Auckland for India. Pappa, in one of his black label highs, accused Ma of sleeping with her work colleague. His obscene choice of words coupled with his drunken voice was enough to make me drag myself out of bed at two in the morning and lash out at him.

It was Ma I was fighting for that night and today it's my unborn child, who is probably tugging at my umbilical cord just a little tighter to feel safe from such ferocity.

Gurveer opens his mouth to say something, but seeing my shivering body he decides to remain silent. He throws a questioning glance at Bi-ji, who lowers her gaze as soon as it meets his. He walks towards me and puts his arm around my shoulders, motioning me to sit down. I'm not sure whether he's doing this for me or because he's worried about his baby. Bi-ji turns her face away, displeased by Gurveer's change of teams. Gurveer looks at me for a few seconds, sighs deeply, then glances at Bi-ji again. He seems uncertain what to say to her. He speaks hesitantly, almost in a murmur, "Bi-ji, what's Priya talking about? What malicious plans?"

"Pooth, I swear on Guru Nanak's name I was only telling Priya pooth to take some traditional medicine for a healthy baby. That's all, and see how she reacts! You saw with your own two eyes, nah? Don't I even have a right to be concerned about her at this time? You tell me, go on, tell tell.

"Enough is enough. "Liar! She's a liar." I raise my voice again and shrug my shoulders away from Gurveer's arm.

"Priya, please calm down yaar," Gurveer begs, this time in a soothing way. "Can't you let Bi-ji be a little concerned at least. She's not your enemy, you know. She only wants what's best for your health."

"Tell him about the milk, huh.Why are you so silent now? go on, tell him about the milk," I say, my stern eyes fixed on Bi-ji, mytone finaland threatening.

Bi-ji hesitates for a few secfonds, then admits to Gurveer about the Medicine Woman and her "magic milk formula".

Gurveer's head hangs low, as though he has beenlet down by his ever-knowing, wise mother. "Bi-ji, you know Priya is not from here, so whyask her to do this? We're not fussed about having a son first anyway. Girl babies are wonderful too. When will you people realise this?" Gurveer stares at hisfmother, sounding disgusted and let down.

Bi-ji glares back at him, her nostrils flaring and her eyes brimming with crocodile tears.She whisks her duppatta across her shoulder and plonks her roughy feet on the floor to leave.

Bi-ji,please sit doen. Let's--," Gurveer says.

"No-no-no," Bi-ji cuts inhastily. "No need! No use talking to my own son who is not mine anymore.Hoon tussi apne kaar ali de thalle lag ke rehna!" Now you are going to live under your wife's rulings.

She marches out of the room with hardly any signs of arthritis.What a superb actress!

Didi hears everything from downstairs but decides against intervening.Her comforting hug some twenty munutes later defrosts the tears that sat frozen inmyveins and allows themto roll down my kohl-seeared eyes.

"Ssh, be strong, Priya,just be strong, sis," she whispers.

Chapter Five

"Watering the Neighbour's Plant"

The PCO/STD phone booth is back in service according to Didi, who made a call to her brother in Germany this morning. "Better call Aunty Kavita," Didi says, wagging her finger at me the way she does when instructing Harpreet and Ranveer to finish their homework.

The phone booth manager greets me with a warm smile and a nod. He quickly hands me the telephone as if he had predicted my arrival. "Please, ma'am, all yours. Shall I dial for you?" He rubs his hands together in a pretend-hand-wash fashion. His grey kurta tunic hangs off his skinny, fair limbs and flaps against his acid-washed jeans. There is no sign of a bum under those jeans - not that I'm checking him out, but it does seem like he's wearing clothes two sizes too big. At least the scarlet turban is a perfect fit and his dark, trimmed moustache sits neatly on his long, thin face. His fluffy beard has been rolled up to his chin, its side ends tucked behind the ears.

"It's okay, Iqbal saab, I'll be fine. Can I please use the other room? It's a bit noisy here." The next room is small but at least there is no background groaning of passing motor-bikes and incessant photocopying machines.

"Sure, sure, all yours. Please." He bows his head slightly.

After a brief moment of dead silence the line resonates with long intermittent beeps. Ma answers in her usual whisper. It's her habit to say hello like a mouse and then gradually increase her volume, depending on the caller and the juiciness of the conversation.

"Hieee, Maaa, it's me - Priya," I squeal like a little girl.

"Long live, beti, how are you? I've been so worried. We are so pleased to hear the great news. I've told your Pappa already that I'm coming over a few weeks before the delivery. Unless of course if you are here by then. O hah, has Gurveer got his visa yet?" Ma rattles off at a thousand miles per hour.

We chat for a few minutes about everything in general and nothing in particular. She dictates a list of do's and don't's for mother and baby. And then she asks the question I've been dreading most.

"So, tell me, is Gurveer's family happy they might have a grandson soon?"

I suck my lips in to force a silence. A quick reply might be hurtful and I don't want to hurt her. My silence continues for a second or so.

"Hello...hello...you still there, beti?" I can hear her tapping her receiver, probably wondering if the line is still connected.

"Yes, Ma, I'm still here. Ma, can I ask you something?"

"Of course, beti, I'm packed with information for mothers-to-be."

"Ma, would you have preferred a boy instead of me?"

"What kind of a silly question is that? Of course, these things are not in a person's hands. It's all fate and God's will," she quips, little realising she is contradicting herself.

"Would you have still had me if you'd known beforehand that your child was going to be another girl?"

"Priya, please - "

"No, please Ma, just answer me. I really need to know."

There is slight irritation in Ma's tone. "Well, I didn't know at the time, did I? I mean, what does it matter anyway? It was so long ago. Why bring all this up now?"

"Stop dodging the question, Ma."

"It's not like technology was advanced like how it is today. It's ridiculous how people are decorating nurseries and buying colour-coordinated clothes and toys for babies who haven't even been born yet. All this scanning business and finding out the sex of the baby is way too advanced for my liking. Where is the surprise element? I mean, really!"

"Ma, I need to know the truth. It's got nothing to do with how much you love me but I still need to know what you would have done had you known beforehand that I was a girl...Ma, Ma...please stop crying..." My voice drowns in Ma's melodramatic metallic sobs. The volume gradually increases and then comes to an abrupt halt.

"What do you think I would have done, Priyanka?" Ma's hostility is obvious in her tone.

"I think I know but I want to hear it from you, Ma."

"Fine, have it your way then. Years I've spent sacrificing my life for you two girls and this is the gratitude I get...No, you be quiet and let me finish - you asked for it and now you must know the truth. My own daughter doubting my intentions. First it's your father's bashings and infidelity - the latter, mind you, is on-going and will probably remain so till he dies. And now it's your stupid cross-examinations. What do you want me to say, Priya? Huh?...I said let me finish. You think my life was a bed of roses like yours is? No, beti, you and Pouja don't know half of it. Yes! Yes, I would have taken remedies to get rid of the baby if I had known. Happy now? But before you start hating me just know one thing…" She pauses briefly. I open my mouth but close it again, not wanting to be told off for the third time.

She resumes amidst sniffles. "Know this - that I love you more than anyone in my entire life. I have loved you unconditionally from the moment I first saw you and counted your ten tiny fingers and ten tiny, chubby toes. I still remember vividly the moment the nurse placed your warm, fragile body, only minutes old, on my chest. You latched on immediately, your fingers clutching onto my forefinger. You opened your eyes and looked straight into mine. That's when I knew that having you was the best thing ever to happen to me…"

My hand and the receiver in it are wet with tears. "Ma, please forgive me, I'm so sorry. I never meant to upset you."

But Ma has hung up.

*****

Two weeks pass and I don't say much to anyone. Gurveer keeps his distance, though I'm not sure if it's to do with his guilt about his mother's behaviour or because he is overwhelmed with the whole idea of parenthood. He comes to bed after I'm sound asleep but somehow I always know when he enters the room. I didn't tell him about my phone call to Ma. Only Didi knows. She realised something was up the moment I entered the front gate.

The children have started studying for their exams. Bi-ji, I hear, isn't speaking to anyone since our fight, not even to Papa-ji. He probably doesn't really care to ask about her silence, not wanting to wreck his much deserved freedom from the world of nagging. Didi and

Pa-ji spend most days making obligatory appearances at weddings. Tara keeps her distance as well. In fact she seems unusually withdrawn, but I don't have the curiosity or inclination to ask her why.

Silence, yoga, reading and my bumble-bee journal become my consolation in these days of quietness.

Today, however, is a good day compared to the last several days. Once again Choudhary Niwas is as still as a graveyard at midnight. I have learned to grab these moments of peace as my solitude. Everyone has gone to yet another wedding of yet another distant relative. In the minimal conversations that we have recently had, Gurveer and I had decided that it was best for me - and a lot safer too - to stay home than to suffer the bumps and dust of the three hour road trip to Ludhiana, Punjab's industrial city. Some say the population and pollution factor in Ludhiana has overtaken that of Delhi, and I hated the pollution there. Though initially I pretend to be upset about being left behind, I'm elated at the idea of having a whole day of alone-time.

I welcome the warmth of a people-free lounge room I haven't entered in the last fortnight. Not even to watch my favourite TV soaps. A glint of sunshine emerges from the light grey sky and dances its kaleidoscopic kathakali dance on the ceiling. No need to switch the fan on today. The late October breeze feels cool on my neck. I toy with the idea of whether I should close the glass louvres or leave them open at a slanting angle. Leaving them open seems more inviting.

I channel surf with the remote control, a plethora of languages, sitcoms, commercials, news, and music videos flash rapidly before me. It's so hard to decide what is more appealing. Maybe the MTV hit parade for now, and later I can flick to the CNN news update.

The MTV video jockey is all bubbly and why wouldn't she be, with a much anticipated Bollywood chick-flick safely tucked under her eighteen-inch waist belt? Her sweet diction introduces me to the hit numbers of this week, counting down to the number one song of the day.

Several minutes pass and some new advertisements appear on the monitor. Indian advertisements are very clever. I particularly like the one where a bright white machine, the god of all washing machines, comes floating down from the sky and lands in a dhobi-ghat. So amazed are the clothes-washers at the divine metal box that they start beating the clothes on the machine instead of the ghat steps for a cleaner, brighter wash!

My concentration on the idiot box is interrupted by a commotion in the outside kitchen. My heart skips a beat as the sound intensifies. Who can it be? Ramu and Raju, under strict instructions from Papa-ji, never come to this side of the house. Besides they've been working for the Choudhary dairy farm for seven years now so they're hardly likely to need any help from me. And it's Tara's day off today. I heard Didi say so this morning when she had to wash all the "big big pots, hai rubba!"

So what is this discreet sound?

An uneasiness creeps up in me. What if Ramu or Raju - or both - are serial killers in hiding and have decided to make me their latest victim after a seven-year break? Or what if someone else knows I'm alone today and wants to harm me? No, I know...what if Bi-ji has stayed back and wants to get me out of her son's life forever by pouring mitti ka tel all over me and burning me alive like the TV soapie mothers-in-law do to their disobeying, not-enough-dowry-bringing daughters-in-law? *C'mon, girl, get real.*

I tip-toe across the lounge and into the inside kitchen. After unlatching the metal hook I bang open the little peek-a-boo window that connects the inside kitchen to the outside one for the hot cooked food to be passed through. I hope the clamorous thud will scare the intruder away. I see no one at first but I can smell smoke. Has someone lit the earthen stove? And then I see her.

Her sari is drenched with mud and the pallu is torn. A small fire, just enough to keep her warm, burns in the earthen stove though there is no pot on it. She sits with her head resting on her folded arms, clutching her knees to her chest. She remains motionless, despite my noise.

For the first time this peek-a-boo window proves useless because I cannot reach out to her. Without latching the hook back in its place, I sprint out of the inside kitchen, through the lounge, through the veranda and into the outside kitchen to her upright, corpselike figure.

"Tara, sweetie, are you okay? What's the matter? Please tell me... No, don't cry, honey... Please don't cry, sweetie. For God's sake, tell me what's wrong. Who did this to you?"

I realise I'm asking way too many questions and not giving her a chance to reply. Her sobs grow louder as I embrace her cold, shivering shoulders and beg her to say something, anything.

"Mem...sahib...I can't even put it in words what he did to Meenaxi...I can't, I can't...all my fault, saala bhen-chod, maa-di-lun, kutta..." she finally mumbles. Tara's blood-shot eyes appear petrified as though a man-eating monster were about to attack her.

"Tara...Tara, please calm down. What happened to Meenaxi?"

Tara takes in a long, deep breath as if this would be her last. She dries her cheeks with the backs of her hands and looks straight into my eyes. I see no more tears, just sheer rage, enough to kill.

She begins, "Memsahib, I suspected all along when he was giving ugly, dirty looks to poor Meenaxi, just because she is not his own like Jyoti and Maya -"

"Who?" Immediately I regret cutting her off like this. "Sorry Tara, I need to know who this man is that you are talking about."

"That bastard husband of mine. Memsahib, you been very upset last few days so I never tell you. That mother's cunt, chutiya, he came back from Canada. They catch him working on a farm. Picking some kind of fruits he tells me. No visa, they told him, go back to your country. He came back nine days ago. All day all night only drinking, drinking, drinking. When I said didn't you bring back any dollars he said it's not my business, not my money to ask him.

"Jyoti always in school when I come to work and Maya and Meenaxi stay home. I don't know how but I can feel when bad things are about to happen. Today morning I tell him I'm going to work and he said go, go, get out. But I lied. I never came to work. I want to see what he does at home. And...and..." Tara's words trail off as she bursts into uncontrollable sobs.

"Say it, Tara, let it out. Don't bottle it up". Tara takes both my hands and grips them in hers tightly, like a lost child. Her shivers return as her tongue finds the courage to let her words out. "I came back inside the house very very quietly. Maya was sleeping but I didn't see Meenaxi. Then I heard her crying softly, my poor poor Meenaxi. I walked fast fast to the toilet where the sound was coming from. He was standing full nanga, no clothes, and forcing his lun inside the poor bacchi's mouth. Chuuso, chuuso, suck, suck, he kept telling her. Then I screamed, Memsahib, I screamed very very very loud. *You Maa-chodh, haraami, what are you doing?* I shout at him. He quickly pushed Meenaxi out of the toilet and locked the door from the inside. He hasn't come out."

My grip on Tara's shoulders vanishes. Like the limbs of a rag doll, my hands land on my knees with a silent thud. Sweet Jesus. What has this animal done to the poor child! My tongue and the walls of my mouth become dry, unable to form words to console Tara. Poor Meenaxi, a small innocent flower bud who is barely six years old, will have to live with this horrific image for the rest of her life. First her mother's untimely death, then her father's abandonment, and now her own uncle forcing his diseased manhood down her fragile throat. How will she ever learn to trust anyone ever again? How easily life has made her girlhood a mere curse.

Be strong, I tell myself. Tara needs you to be strong. I stroke Tara's hair and wipe her smeared cheeks. "Tara, let's go to the police. That bastard, fucking son-of-a-bitch. You can't let him get away with this."

Tara shakes her head profusely. "Nahi, nahi, Memsahib," she begs. "I can't tell police. We are poor people. This happens in so many poor people's homes. They won't take me seriously. And after all, he is my husband. I can't destroy my own house. All my fault anyway. Never should have brought Meenaxi home. Hai bhagwaan, what will I tell my sister when I die?"

I refuse to believe the submissive vile pouring out of Tara's mouth. Is it my imagination or has Tara just dismissed the whole horrific act as a household norm?

There is a burning sensation in my throat like I've swallowed a handful of chilli powder. I want to spit out fire but instead I manage to only yell,"Tara, this is NOT your fault! A good husband is your other half, your life partner, not a criminal you must keep in hiding. This man is dangerous! You have to report what he's done. What the fuck are you protecting him for? He has given you nothing but hell over the last few years. Look at you, working day and night to feed and clothe your kids, to save up for their dowry. And what's he done? Nothing! Takes off to Canada, never once thinking what will become of you and the kids. Doesn't send home money. Drinks day and night. And don't hide it anymore, I'm not stupid - I know he rapes you as well. And now this inhumane act on Meenaxi. How can you blame yourself for all this? Thank God you caught him. Yet even after all this you don't want to go to the police! Why, Tara, why?"

Tara's silence is making me sick to my stomach. She sits still, taking in all that I'm dishing out at her. I don't know what she's thinking. Here is a woman who is independent, yet fearful of what society will say. She fears a system that has taught her, and many others like her, to suffer. For in suffering lies a woman's honour.

This has to stop. I grab her by the shoulders and shake her. "Tara, you can make a difference. You don't have to be afraid of anything or anyone."

"But, Memsahib, who will marry my daughters if their father is in jail? Memsahib, what would you do if you were in my place?"

"I'd cut his fucking dick off, that's what I'd do!"

"Dick?"

"Yes, dick, penis - lun, or whatever else you guys call it here!"

"Memsahib, forgive me, I know you are very angry because I don't want to go to police. I tried to kill myself, jumped into the river, but I know how to swim.

Even Yamraj doesn't want me up there yet! Memsahib, give me a few more days and I will think about it. Please. Life here is very hard for women. Nobody cares, nobody listens. If I go to a policeman maybe he will want me to lift my knees up for him. If I go to my family they will only say, "See, we told you he was a good-for-nothing chamaar." Memsahib, don't be angry. You Kiwi and everything easy in phoren, but here not so easy. Here it's a curse to be a woman."

She gathers her tattered sari and stands up. Before she leaves she gazes at me with moist eyes and says, "Please don't tell anyone about this, Memsahib. I came here only to tell you. I know nobody else is home today - that's why I come. Please don't even tell Gurveer Pa-ji."

With that she walks briskly into the hustle and bustle of the hawker-infested main street. The afternoon sun is once again performing its kathakali dance but I stand oblivious to any peripheral sounds or visions of hope and happiness. No TV sitcom or commercial, no novel, no journal-writing, and certainly no food is going to give me what I so desperately want right now. To cry. To cry real loud. To scream.

I want to mourn for Tara, for Meenaxi, for every woman in India, or maybe for every woman in the world and the choices we make. And sometimes do not make.

*****

Gurveer's daily excursions to faraway village weddings without me is beginning to test my patience. I know he doesn't really enjoy these occasions but at least he gets to wear nice clothes. Meanwhile I'm stuck at home in my boring salwaar kameezes. So many saris and lehengas, all untouched, swathed in tissue paper and neatly arranged on top of each other in the king sized bed-box.

It's not that Gurveer doesn't want to take me with him, but my morning sickness - and I don't know why it's called that because it rarely occurs in the mornings - hinders me from enjoying the food and drinks and sweets at these weddings. And my back starts to hurt sitting in the car for too long during the winding trip.

Just when I lose all hope of ever attending a lavish wedding in a nice big marriage palace, an invitation arrives accompanied by a red, green and gold glitter and a tinsel-embellished box of bundi laddo - my favourite sweetmeat.

It's been two days since Tara confided in me about her paedophile husband. I hope she comes to her senses soon and gets the police to arrest the sick bastard. Better still, hang him.

Tara hasn't come to work since that horrible afternoon and the house workload is beginning to take its toll on Didi's ever-strong, un-drooping shoulders. She refuses to let me help and insists I rest and enjoy this blissful time in my life.

But today I insist on making lunch for everyone. Usually Didi debates with me for even the little things I want to lend a hand with, like peeling the potatoes or chopping the onions for the curry tarka, but seeing my enthusiasm, she gives in.

"The smells don't make me sick any more. I swear, Didi, I'll be fine. You've got to let me cook every now and then, otherwise Ma's years of hard work in teaching me to roll perfectly round rotlis - sorry, that's Gujrati for rotis - will go to waste," I tease her.

"Fine, but you mustn't strain yourself. No lifting the ghee bucket - I'll get that down for you. And no bending down too low. Okay?" she orders.

"Yes, Major Paramjeet Kaur," I salute, and give her a quick hug.

She winks at me and hands me the round, steel spice box. Lifting the glass lid, I smell the pungent aroma of spices. It's been ages since I let my fingers touch these magic ingredients that turn simple parts of plants into sumptuous curries.

I busy myself dicing purple onions and within seconds I'm wiping my teary eyes with the corner of my duppatta. I'm about to discreetly sniff out a little snot into the chiffon fabric when I'm startled by a thin figure appearing in the kitchen like a fast-courier apparition.

"Hi Bhabi-ji," she greets me with her eighteen-year-old smile. Her skin as flawless as the girls in the fairness-cream advertisements, she appears confident in her five-foot-tall slenderness, clad in a Jaipuri yellow salwaar kameez with tiny mirrors on her cotton duppatta.

"Oh hi, Manjeet," I say. "How are you sweetie? Long time no see."

Manjeet Kaur is Gurveer's distant cousin from his mother's side. She lives two parallel streets away from Choudhary Niwas, in her parents' beige marble mansion, lovingly named by them Chopra Cottage. She comes from a filthy rich Punjabi family, well balanced with two sons and two daughters. Eldest son first (but of course), then daughter, then daughter again, and finally, after fifteen years, a big, fat boy baby whom everyone affectionately calls Sethi, meaning princely.

"I'm great, Bhabi. Sorry I haven't come by. Been really busy with exams. I'm going to sit the pre-medical exam next week. Fingers crossed, nah. And now suddenly this wedding. You remember Tej, nah?" she asks, her words pouring out in a speed as though she's on a timed impromptu speech contest.

It's a breath of fresh air to see a vibrant, fashionable teenager on a day like today when although I've been trying to appear cheerful, my mind restless with Tara's gruesome descriptions. "Of course I remember Tejinder, very sweet girl. What about her?" I ask politely.

Manjeet and her older sister Tejinder have been quite fond of me since they met me at my wedding. They were overjoyed to have a sister-in-law who was a foreigner. Coming from a family with money growing in their backyard, these girls are quite up-to-date with fashion, boys and Western culture - all courtesy of cable TV and glossy magazines.

"Guess what?" she continues, interlacing her pencil-thin fingers together, "Tej is getting married tomorrow! Yah, I know, such short notice, nah? But we had to do everything chut-putt....ring ceremony was last night. Sorry, huh, we didn't invite anyone because it was arranged so quickly. And Tej's hubby-to-be, my Jijju-ji yaar, only arrived from the UK yesterday morning. His family came over for afternoon chai and ek dum, everything was fixed. Jijju-ji has to go back to London next week so he wants to marry ASAP. My dear Tej didi is right now getting mehandi done on her hands and I'm rushing around like mad handing out these invites to everyone."

She pauses, catches her breath. "Verrrry basic card, nothing fancy - no time, yaar. Here you go - oh and the bundi laddoo too." She finally finishes what seemed like a three minute ad lib speech and hands me the shimmery box. The accompanying invitation card is indeed a rather plain red folded one with just a Sikh khanda symbol imprinted in the centre.

This card's plainness must really be bothering Chopra Uncle. I'm sure he has instructed Manjeet to apologise about its nakedness to every single person she hands one to. I mean, really, with so much wealth surely Chopra Sardar Ji would be expected to get a decent card for her eldest daughter's wedding invite.

In bright bold red letters on a boring white background it says:

Tejinder Kaur Chopra weds Dharam Veer Singh

I realise I finally have a wedding I can go to! "Wow, this is great. I'll have to go and dig out what to wear. Thanks, Manjeet."

"Oh, more than welcome, Bhabi. By the way, where's Param Bhabi and Maasi-ji?"

"Right here, my dear," Didi replies, startling us both with her abrupt appearance. She pecks a kiss on Manjeet's cheek. "Your Maasi-ji has gone to satsang...again," she says, displaying her tongue-in-cheek grin.

"Hi, Bhabi, it's Tej's wedd -"

"I know, I heard everything from outside. How wonderful! She's too lucky to find a UK catch. Kismat, yaar!" Didi prods Manjeet in her ribs. "Does your Jijju-ji have..." any younger brother or boy cousin to fix you up with? Huh, huh? Go on, tell tell! See how she blushes!"

Didi untangles the gold thread tied securely around the sweet-box. She takes a chunky bite off one of the eleven daffodil-yellow laddoos and lazily hands me the box with one hand while licking the gooey fingers of the other. Gleefully I snatch the box from her and satisfy my aroused tastebuds.

"Anyway, Bhabi-jis, see you at the palace tomorrow," Manjeet says. "Gotta rush. Bye."

We wave her goodbye with our sticky, delicious fingers.

The wedding excitement keeps my mood in check for the rest of the day. I finish cooking my bhindi sabji and head upstairs to rummage through my bed-box for all the glitter and glamour of Indian haute couture that I can wear without showing too much of my growing belly.

*****

A large crowd has already gathered in the lawns of Laali Farms Marriage Palace. I realise we are a little late, although it's no big deal in this part of the world to arrive late at weddings. It is fashionably termed "Indian timing" whereby if the invite says ten a.m. it really means one p.m. and if it says one p.m it really means five p.m and so on. Thankfully our late arrival doesn't raise any eyebrows.

The venue is a melting pot of colour, spicy aromas and chatter. Multi-coloured turbans bob in the air like excited butterflies. Sari pallus and salwaar kameez duppatas graze the green manicured lawns like a soft ocean breeze. Rich, spoilt little brats run around carefully laid tables and scream at the tops of their lungs, demanding more - more samousas, more fruit-chaat, more gulab-jamun, more jalebi, more gajrella, more chum-chums, more pakoras. And even more oily food, fried in the same pan of oil for the hundredth time, contributing to the morning-after stomach cramps followed by stinging pee-like shitting.

I take small, elegant steps, extra careful not to trip over my lehenga-choli. Out of the glory box Ma had prepared for me, I had picked out a netted fabric fitted blouse, lavender-coloured, with a matching heel-length skirt, the satin lining underneath accentuating a slimming flow. I took full advantage of the occasion and

decided to wear my kundan wedding jewellery -
precious pearl-like gems set in twenty-two carat gold,
though my accessories are minimal compared to the
flashing gold and diamonds in this crowd of at least two
thousand people.

To think that Tej's wedding was arranged only a
few days ago is almost unconceivable when one sees
the number of heads wobbling and mouths eating
away. And this is just outside. Inside the palace there're
even more.

Green plastic chairs - hundreds of them - are
neatly assembled in a gigantic hall. Most seats are
occupied by people whose eyes are glued to the centre
stage entertainment area. Live singers, bhangra dancers,
and a slim-waisted girl with a bare midriff who mimes
the words to Bollywood film songs and re-enacts replica
dance moves.

Below the stage is the dance platform for people to
make merry and shake a leg - or in a seriously Punjabi
sense shake the shoulders. Though the dance floor is
open to all ages and both genders, women refrain from
entering this alcohol-high zone. Children are indifferent
to the stench of imported whisky or the embarrassing,
uncoordinated bhangra jerks by men who are under a
deranged misconception that the bare-midriff girl will be
finding them incredibly sexy.

Luckily we find some vacant seats in the third
row from the back. Our views of the dancing loonies
aren't that great but we don't complain. At least the
entertainment stage is high up so everyone can get a
good look at it. On the extreme right corner of the hall
is another little stage occupied by two vintage-looking
thick-armed sofas. These scarlet-velvet upholstered
chairs are decorated with silk cushions. Behind them is

a wall embellished with marigolds, orchids and roses. A large placard pasted amongst the flower arrangement reads:

Congratulations Dharam Veer and Tejinder.

I stare at the extravagance of the decorations. Indeed Chopra Uncle has managed to put up a fine party for his little girl. Now everyone can shut up about the plain, ordinary invitation cards!

The Choudhary men decide to leave we women and children on our own and flock off to mingle with their species. After much pestering from Rannu and Preetu, Didi accompanies them outside to bring us back some finger-licking (but later diarrhoea-evoking) fried food. Bi-ji sits three seats away from me and avoids looking my way. Instead she finds some lady beside her to discuss the half nakedness and the revolting pelvic thrusts of the "nanga" dancing girl.

"What took you so long? I'm starving!" I let out a genuine cry of hunger to Didi as she places on my lap two plates of pakoras with tamarind chutney smeared on them.

For some time now I've been noticing a group of women who are constantly looking at me and whispering in each others ears. I glance at my shoulders to see if perhaps my bra strap is showing. No. Then I examine my crossed knees to see if maybe my Elle Macphersen Intimates knickers are showing. Again no. Giving up, I tilt my neck towards Didi's head and whisper, "Why are those women staring at me? Do I look okay? I don't think they like what I'm wearing."

Didi hadn't seen them as yet but she looks in the direction of this village-women clique. It's difficult for Didi to speak over the blaring Punjabi remix numbers coming out of the nearby speakers so she grabs my arm and says, "Let's go to the washroom. There's something I need to tell you."

*****

We stand in front of the mirrors in the ladies' toilets, waiting for the teeny boppers in their bra top lehenga choli suits to float out of the room before Didi can tell me this "something" she needs to tell me.

"Well?" I say with much impatience in my tone.

"Those women are from Balwinder's in-law's side," she eventually says.

Balwinder was Gurveer's only sister, Bi-ji and Papa-ji's eldest child. No one speaks about Balwinder much, not even Gurveer. She didn't come to our wedding so I've yet to meet her. Gurveer simply dismissed the whole thing as some "family problem" when I asked him how come she never came to her baby brother's wedding. Since no one ever mentioned her name at home in time I forgot all about her. Until now.

"So?" I ask, puzzled. "That still doesn't explain why they keep staring at me. Shouldn't they be staring at Bi-ji instead?"

Didi opens her mouth, then pauses for a few seconds as if weighing in her mind whether it's a good idea to say the words she's holding back.

"C'mon, yaar," I say. "It's not like I've done or said anything to Balwinder. I don't even know her." I'm certain Didi is making a mistake - these women are probably wondering why I'm wearing a mosquito net for an outfit!

"If you must know," Didi hesitantly lets her words out, "before Gurveer met you Bi-ji and Papa-ji had agreed to reserve his hand in marriage to Simran, Balwinder's husband's youngest sister. She's three years younger than Gurveer."

I stare at her, dumbfounded by this new revelation.

"Stop gawking at me like that. It happens here all the time, yaar - too common." Didi elbows me. She's right - one brother-sister set marrying another brother-sister set happens a lot in Punjab. It has been an age-old practice to save dowry, since both families are giving their daughter away to their respective sons. There's also an unspoken understanding that there will not be any future demands or threats for dowry, the underlying principle being, "If you hurt my daughter we'll hurt yours!"

"Okay, fine. So they're just pissed off that Gurveer married me instead of this young, sweet, innocent, fair n lovely, same caste girl! I really don't give a shit, man. And here I thought my knickers were showing." I abandon my poor efforts at concealing my jealousy. Something in Didi's saddened eyes tells me there is more to know.

She takes the edge of the bottle-green kashmiri shawl she is wearing over her emerald silk salwaar suit and dabs at the tears forming in the corner of her eyes, careful not to smudge her eyeliner. "The day Balwinder's husband and in-laws found out about you and Gurveer, poor Balwinder was forbidden to have anything to do with any of us ever again. Not even Bi-ji and Papa-ji."

Didi's attempts to control her tears is turning somewhat futile as she begins to openly sob. "Priya," she says, "we haven't seen Balwinder for the last three years. None of us. They told her to choose between her parents' home and them."

And she obviously chose her "real home", I want to say but don't. So much like my poor Ma, who suffered

ill-treatments from her mother-in-law and bashings from
my father, and yet never left her "real home"

"That's why she didn't come to our wedding
then?" I ask.

"Yes. Not just her, but her husband's entire family
- even the distant ones, like the ladies you saw inside
gossiping about you."

"But, Didi, can't they just get over it? What's the
big deal? Isn't there anyone else who can marry
Balwinder's sister-in-law? Besides, it's not like Gurveer
betrayed her. I don't think he was even told about all
this, right?" I desperately cross my fingers for a
favourable response.

"You're right, Priya, Gurveer didn't know. But,
my dear sister, in this part of the world marriages are
arranged by parents and only later are the children told
about it. I wrote to Gurveer about it but it was too late.
By then he had already met you."

So it was all my fault then! I stole Bi-ji and Papa-
ji's youngest prince and made him mine when in fact he
was promised to a girl who would have probably not
only brought more dowry than I ever did (well, I
brought none actually!), but would have also given them
a pure-blood grandson.

Didi's words evoke an uncomfortable muteness in
me. All I manage is a few sounds of deep sighing. As if
putting a formal closure to the discussion, Didi excuses
herself to use a cubicle which conveniently becomes
available after a masculine-looking female hurries out of
it. It takes a several seconds for me to realise that this
person is indeed a male dressed in women's clothing.

I try and swallow my bitter saliva mixed with anger
and possessiveness. The harder I try not to let all this
affect me, the more painful my throat becomes. After a

few seconds I take a deep breath and deviate my attention to the person using the vanity mirror next to me.

She/He walks, or rather floats on tiptoes, to the imposing vanity mirrors hanging on the betel-stained pink walls. Wearing a broad smile she examines the whiteness of the teeth, making sure to wipe off any smudged red lipstick stains. A quick squeeze in of the cheeks and a pout like Madam Rekha, Bollywood's famous pout. She carefully examines the right cheek, then left, blusher seems perfect. Now the mascara - she flutters the extra-long eyelashes like a Cheshire cat on heat. Hot pink eyelids complement the fuchsia zardozi work salwaar kameez. After giving a final look of approval to the reflection, she turns around and breaks into a thousand watt smile. She realises I've been staring openly at this exquisite display of a eunuch hijra glamour.

She flicks the manicured nails - flick, flick, flick - then extends her right hand to me while the left arm hangs in the air, bent at the elbow, as though in an invisible sling. In a husky voice comes a "Hi there. The name's Sanjana Singh. What's yours?"

I'm taken aback at the impeccable English of my new found friend. Well, I'm hoping she will consider being my friend. I realise how much I miss my gay friends in Auckland who were always there for me "rain or hail, sweetie". Although, unlike with Tammy, my wee-hour K-Road café visits with them were mostly to listen to endless stories about their new boyfriends who had left them because they got so drunk at someone's party that they ended up bedding an ex-lover!

I return Sanjana's smile with an equally bright one and shake her hand. "I'm Priyanka…Priyanka Patel, but call me Priya. Nice to meet you."

"The pleasure's mine, darrrling. Now tell me, do I look all right? I mean, seriously, I don't look too fat in this Punjabi suit now, do I? It's not always I wear this traditional stuff, you know. I prefer my Ritu Beri jeans and Sabyasachi kaftaans, they are oh-so-comfy!"

I recognise these Indian designers' names immediately, thanks to my religious devotion to reading the fortnightly issues of *Femina* magazine from cover to cover. Ritu Beri has to be India's most popular fashion talent, making her mark in Paris, and the success of Sabyasachi's designs at the Lakme India Fashion Week would give other hot shot designers a run for their money.

Someone once said, "Never tell a woman she looks fat." I have to admit Sanjana is not exactly fat, but she could do with a few sit-ups. Her waist is thick though not flabby and her chest seems to have way too many rolled tissues stuck disproportionately on each boob. And I really think my gay friend Stuart, had he been here at this moment, would have dragged this drag to the nearest beauty salon for a full body wax. I could easily braid the ringlets covering Sanjana's arms.

"Not at all, Sanjana. You look absolutely gorgeous." I lie, but only slightly. She does have attractive facial features - a thin, long nose, smooth skin (no stubble), huge dark eyes and full Shah-Rukh-Khan lips.

"Like Kareena Kapoor?" she asks, referring to one of Bollywood's glamour girls.

"Spot on," I reply, my smile still wide.

The flushing in Didi's cubicle resonates within the pink room. Startled, Sanjana cries, "Uff, I didn't realise there was someone in there." Then she sees Didi and jumps with joy, like she's found a long lost friend. "Hi,

Param darrrling, tussi kidda, my dear? Haven't seen you for so long!"

I'm glad to see Didi's face lighting up when she recognises Sanjana. Memories of Balwinder had clearly upset her.

"Oh, hi, Sanjeev. How've you been? Here, meet my sister-in-law, Priya."

"Yaar, don't call me Sanjeev, puhleese! It breaks my heart when people call me that. I'm like you girls, no? Darrrling, please call me Sanjana only, okay? And yes, I have met Priyanka...Priya, did you say?" She turns her gaze at me. "She's a sweetheart! Do you know what? She reckons I look like Kareena Kapoor!"

The uncomfortable thickness that had lurked in the air a few minutes ago evaporates as the three of us busy ourselves admiring each other's outfits and accessories.

Sanjana rummages through her burgundy leather handbag and pulls out a business card. Handing me the card, she proudly announces, "Here, Priya, I work for the Punjab Hijra NGO. That's my mobile number, and below that is my home one. Call me sometime, accha." Her candyfloss nails graze the plastic coated card as she points out the numbers printed on it in a curly font. The B.A., LL.B. and M.A. (Women's Lit) credentials appearing under her name on the card confirms my suspicions that Sanjana is not just another wedding singer-dancer eunuch.

"What sort of work do you do, Sanjana?" I ask, curious and elated to make a gay friend in India, someone to email my other gay mates back home about.

"Well, we fight for equal rights for the hijra community. We also collaborate with other feminist NGOs and work towards providing education for the poor, especially girls who'd been pulled out of school so their brothers can get an education instead. And we help battered and homeless women and children. You know, Priya, so many Indian women live in silence about their abusive, drunkard husbands. Our work is to make these women realise they're not alone."

"Wow, that's so great. You must love your job - it sounds so fulfilling," I say with admiration. Finally I meet someone who's standing up for women's rights. I'm tempted to blurt out my concerns for Tara, but remembering Tara's promise and also because Didi is present, I decide to say nothing.

"I do, I love my job - so if you wanna donate, give me a call. We NGOs are desperate for community support, financial and in kind. Param here has been very generous by donating litres and litres of milk every time we have a charity function," says Sanjana, pinching Didi's cheek.

A sudden loud knock on the door startles us. No woman would be knocking on the ladies' restroom door. Must be a man. Sanjana flings open the door to be faced with Pa-ji, who seems to have been looking for Didi and me.

"Tussi? Ki hoya, ji?," asks a rather shocked Didi, asking him what happened.

"Come on, we're leaving," says Pa-ji. He appears serious and concerned.

Didi gives me and Sanjana a surprised glance and turns back to face Pa-ji.

"But, Harpreet-de-Daddy, the wedding hasn't even started."

It really annoys me when she calls him Harpreet's daddy. I feel like telling her, The man has a name, it's Jasveer Choudhary - use it, woman! Hardly any woman

I know in Punjab calls her husband by his proper name, because each time she does her husband's life span is significantly reduced. She can call him "Aji sunte ho" - O, thou please listen to thee - or use any other reference to denote their marital connection. Many times I hear women in bazaars calling their husbands "Raju ke papa" or "Meena ke daddy" or "Veeru ke bapu". Bi-ji has often scowled at hearing me call Gurveer by his first name. The chance of me calling him "Harpreet's uncle" was as far-fetched as Bi-ji shaving her legs. Never.

Pa-ji shakes his head with despair and says, "Doesn't look like there'll be a wedding any more. There's some dowry disagreement going on. The groom's side is threatening to leave. C'mon let's go."

I can hardly believe my ears. Dowry disagreement? No way, this can't be. Isn't Chopra Uncle the richest Sardar in Hoshiarpur City? This drama is worth a peek, I decide.

Sure enough, the paved entrance courtyard is buzzing with two distinctly demarcated groups of people - one with heads high up, turbans sky-high and stiff, chests right out and noses flagged up in the air, obviously the groom's side. The other group is exactly the opposite - drooped shoulders, heads hung low and arms folded.

A man, whom Didi identifies as "patchola"-the middleman who arranged the match whispers something into Chopra Uncle's ears, listens to his whispered reply, then bobs along to kowtow to the high-and-mighty father of the groom. We watch him continue his little message delivering saga like a ping pong ball being tossed from one side of the court to the other. Finally the small, plump messenger places his hands on his waist and puts on a diplomatic-cum-apologetic-cum-

"I'm pissed off, let's just get on with this marriage" look and says loud enough to Chopra Uncle so we are able to hear his clever suggestion, "Sar ji, it's only another twenty lakhs more they want. Paghdi in question, Sar ji."

Chopra Uncle's face mellows as he lets the craft of emotional blackmail work its wonder. Paghdi, the Sikh turban, symbolises honour and Chopra Uncle isn't about to lose his honour. So often the bride's father is left with no choice but to take his turban off and place it at the groom's father's feet, begging the other man to accept his daughter and continue with the marriage ceremony.

It's clear this isn't about the money. That he has plenty of. Everyone knows that on the night of the ring ceremony a truckload of dowry was delivered to the groom's father - one brand new Suzuki Maruti car for the groom's father, one brand new Kinetic scooter for the groom's younger brother, twenty tole pure gold (each tola is ten grams), forty tole pure silver, a fridge, TV, washing machine, microwave, and a bank cheque of twenty-one lakh rupees.

And now the beast demands a further twenty lakhs in cash for this son who has a shiny, navy UK passport "or else the wedding is off!" Quickly I calculate and it comes to a whopping figure of seventy thousand New Zealand dollars!

Had Gurveer's father ever demanded all this from my Pappa - not that he would have, and I'm also quite certain Gurveer wouldn't have hung his sehra covered face low like this daddy's-arse-kissing Dharam Veer - my thrifty father would gladly have told them to "piss off" in his most polite Gujrati accent. After all, he is a scrooge, a money-loving Patel.

Several minutes pass while the bridal party congregates in a corner to consider the last and final bid.

Finally Chopra Uncle fishes his cell phone out from his kurta tunic's side pocket and punches a few numbers. He whispers instructions to someone, but we can't hear him. Then he hangs up and whispers something into the patchola's ear. The messenger smiles widely and hops along to the groom's party with the latest update. Several more minutes pass.

Didi pokes her elbow into my ribs and points to a white Mercedes pulling into the marigold-embellished driveway. "He's here. Arre, Harjinder yaar, Tej's brother, the older one. Look, look, I think he's got the money. See, I told you, nah?"

The spectators stand gawking while mission-accomplished grins appear on the faces of the groom's party.

"How come though? In just like twenty minutes only?" I ask, looking at my watch, amazed.

"Black money yaar. These rich people all have it in their little grey metal safe somewhere in their house."

Didi is right. Harjinder opens the black attaché case to display the crisp hundred rupee notes neatly stapled and stacked on top of each other. They look exactly like the kind the Bollywood movies have when the heroine's father gives ransom money to the bad daaku kidnapper. Though in the movies a hunky hero always ends up rescuing his heroine girlfriend, booting the attaché case in the air so the notes fly down a huge mountain like confetti, kicking the kidnapper's arse, and ofcourse winning the heroine's father's heart, who had hated him all along until then.

But poor Tej has no hero to show up to draw his kirpan and save her from this business deal which everyone so conveniently terms marriage. Indeed a business deal it is for how else did Chopra Uncle find a son-in-law who is not only rich but an NRI - non-resident Indian - a status that supposedly brings with it prestige and honour.

The briefcase is politely handed over by the middleman to the high-chested party, and the bridal party resumes the celebrations, the entire crowd once again happy and joyous. Music blares out and arms are flying in the air as people dance to it. Hugs, hugs and more hugs are exchanged to congratulate the two men - one who held on to the honour of his turban and the other whose brilliant negotiation skills got him a fine price for his son.

I spot Gurveer chatting with Pa-ji and Didi. They wave at me to join them back in the hall for lunch. Sanjana gets lost in the crowd, and with her my hopes to befriend her. No one seems to be at all affected by what just happened. Except me.

I say a silent prayer for Tej. O Ganesha, bless Tej with a happy married life. Let her not see the evil that lurks in the homes in foreign countries. Let her not suffer beatings from her husband, nor ill-treatment from her in-laws, nor the temptations of the West. Make her strong and let her remember her true identity. Bless her with good friends like Tammy. Bless her always, O Ganesha.

*****

Just as I enjoy dressing up for wedding parties, I despise taking off the jewellery - dozens and more bangles - the weighty duppatta and the heavy make-up.

It's late afternoon. The ladies of the house decided to return earlier than the men, though Gurveer said he wouldn't be too late. He was going to catch up with some former high school friends who had come to Tej's wedding that he hadn't seen for years.

I slip off the last of my glass bangles when the chrome knob of our bedroom door turns. It's Bi-ji.

For the last fortnight the only words I have uttered to her are my peiri peynas in the mornings, and like a broken record she utters back her usual blessing, "Jinda reh".

She smiles as she enters the room and the kindness on her face raises a pang of guilt in my throat. I feel awful that I haven't made the first move to restore peace in our relationship. Since I'm younger it's my duty to ask for forgiveness, or at least start a polite conversation.

"Bi-ji, aa jao. Are you feeling okay?" I enquire gently.

"Yes, pooth, I'm fine. Can I talk to you?" she says, her tone firm but polite.

"Of course. What is it?" I motion her to sit on the bed, next to me.

"Pooth, you saw what happened today to Chopra-Ji, Tej's papa?" she asks, her eyes looking deep into mine, her voice low and serious.

"Yes, Bi-ji. That was awful. I thought I was the only one upset, but you too, nah? I can't believe that devil demanded more dowry. He should be arrested for it."

"Priya, today you saw what happens to most girls and their fathers during a wedding. This is not uncommon." She pauses, concern in her eyes. "Pooth, this is the reason people in India don't want daughters. Chopra-Ji is lucky, he is a rich man. But think of the poor people. They can't escape from this ongoing dowry system and the police don't help.

There is a saying in this country, pooth, that 'having a daughter is like watering a neighbour's plant'. You feed her, clothe her, educate her, invest in her, but at last she is paraaya dhan, a stranger's possession. She goes to her real home, to her husband, to his family. After that we parents don't even take one sip of water from her."

I want to interrupt her and open my mouth to say something, but my guilty pangs demand that I shut up and let my elderly ma-in-law say her piece.

She continues, "Priya pooth, do you want this sort of thing to happen to us? Think about it. We already have Harpeet's dowry to save up for. Please don't be angry with me, pooth. I only want what's best for us."

She hangs her head low and sighs heavily. Seeing my silence, she says grimly, "The pundit told me that another girl in this house might prove bad luck for us. Please pooth, there is nothing wrong with the milk formula. It tastes like normal milk, trust me." She pauses and waits for my reply.

God, not again! I don't want another argument so I take a deep breath to calm my bubbling anxiety and focus on the best possible response I can give her. As much as I want to lash out at her again, something inside me holds me back. I can feel defeat pouring slowly through my veins and in and out of the chambers of my heart.

"Bi-ji," I say, trying to keep my cool, "I know you mean well but I don't know if I can do this for you. Please understand."

"I do understand, pooth, believe me I do. There's no harm in trying the milk. I'm not asking you to harm the baby. This is my grandchild and I am proud of him. Just try it, please. Will you think about it at least? Please, I beg you."

"Bi-ji, can I ask you something?"

Her eyes light up. "Anything pooth." She probably wasn't expecting me to be this calm.

"Bi-ji, why is it so important to have a son? Look at all the things that girls have achieved today. And look at you, Bi-ji. You have single-handedly transformed a barren piece of land into a flourishing dairy farm. Papa-ji never tires of praising your business sense. And there are women who are in such high positions - one of the wisest leaders of India was a woman."

Bi-ji sucks her bottom lip and stares back expressionlessly, as though debating with herself whether or not she should acknowledge the great achievements of her womenfolk. I take advantage of her silence to continue my attempt at making her realise our true worth.

"Remember how proud you were when Kalpana Chawla, our first ever Indian-born woman in space, went on TV to talk about her next mission? Bi-ji, she was just an ordinary girl from an ordinary village in Haryana and look at the extraordinary life she has. She is the epitome of courage, determination, and dedication for every Indian girl. Please, Bi-ji, you can't say that you have totally given up on our gender. You, me…we are one. We must stand by each other for each other. No one else will."

She closes her heavy eyelids to allow the brimming tears to roll freely down her blemished cheeks. "It's not as simple as you think, pooth. Life has many hurdles and these hurdles are not the same for every individual nor every nation. Being a woman in India is a lot tougher than in New Zealand or any other Western country. Here we live by religious and customary expectations. We must conform to the society in which we live. There you Westerners do not worry about what your neighbour wears or eats or drinks. Here we make sure we know what people in the next village are up to. It is these customary practices that force our society to hail the boy child and condemn the girls. We women do not have an identity. We are merely given a secondary status. I know what I went through as a young girl and then later as a wife and a mother. Life is never fair, Priya pooth, and in life one must not deliberately repeat one's mistakes. My mistake was being born a woman. I do not want my daughters and you to make the same mistake with your offspring. Can you imagine bringing another girl into this harsh world of emotional slavery where every whim of the male gender must be satisfied? Where every moment is dedicated to someone else - husband, children, in-laws - and never once to yourself?"

Her sobs become louder. She takes the end of her pallu and blows her nose, her garnet and gold nose stud twitching. I can't help but wonder whether these tears are a convincing gimmick or if they are truly coming from a concerned mother-in-law who is so sick of her country's system that she will go to any desperate measures to ensure she has a grandson.

"Please, pooth, please do this for me."

"I'll think about it, Bi-ji, I promise."

"Good girl...very, very good girl," she says and hugs me. She picks herself up from the bed and walks towards the door. For a moment she hesitates, but then she turns around to face me. Her face erupts into a warm smile. "Thank you."

I sink into my bed and breathe deeply into the thick air of victory Bi-ji has left behind. I feel defeated and I don't know how it happened. Well, it's only milk, I tell myself. It can't be that bad.

Later in the night, as Gurveer lies on my lap after making love with much satiety, I yearn to tell him about

Bi-ji's second attempt at getting me to take the milk formula. Before I say anything he asks me about Sanjana.

"Yeah, she's really cool." I adjust my back against the velvet-padded bedhead. "Have you spoken to her before?"

"No, and why do you keep calling him her?"

"Because she prefers it that way…her real name's not even Sanjana, it's Sanjeev. She reminds me of Stuart. God, I miss them all."

Gurveer gives me a look as if I had just told him I was gay too. He was a bit too homophobic to be comfortable about my gay friends but he never actually minded me having them. He must have been a little jealous because he kept reminding me that Stuart and the rest still had male bodies. That's something I totally ignored because I liked their girlie habits and found I could click with them, the same way I had with Sanjana.

Something odd crosses my mind. "Jaanu," I say, "imagine the joy Sanjana's family must have felt when she was born, a boy outside - yet inside she was really a girl."

"Well, that's how it is, isn't it? Everyone rejoices when a son is born. How were they to know he was going to turn out to be a hijra!"

"But it's something to think about. I mean, all this hoo ha about having a son, and the big celebrations when they get one, only to find out some years later that he prefers to lead a girl's life. I wonder if her parents still speak to her."

"Most of them get disowned by their families when they admit they're gay."

I shake my head and sigh deeply. "That's so unfair. That's why so many hijras don't have any choice but to dance at weddings and other functions to make ends meet. But you know, Sanjana is very educated. I'm not sure how she would have managed that. Must have been so hard."

Gurveer's eyelids slowly droop and I decide to spare him any further boredom. But this is a good time to bring up the milk formula. I stir him awake and tell him everything Bi-ji said to me that evening.

He listens attentively, and nods as I relate Bi-ji's explanation about the fear of dowry and all. Then he takes my hand from his forehead and kisses it gently. "Will you do it?" he asks.

"Dunno. It's so hard to explain to Bi-ji that this is all just some stupid superstition. Jaanu, I have full faith in God and I know that whatever he gives us is what I'll give birth to. Boy or girl doesn't matter. And no specially formulated milk or a bloody boy-doll bestowed to a deity will change the sex of a baby."

Gurveer knows about Ma's foolish attempts to change me into a boy while I was still floating in her belly. He also knows about how when Ma went into labour no one held her hand except Daksha Aunty. And how no one except seven-year-old Pouja accompanied by Daksha Aunty came to see the new baby once word got out that I was not a boy. My father even disappeared for a while, not coming home again until a week after I was born. According to Ma his pores were oozing with alcohol.

Gurveer notices my mood turning as dark as my irises and places his hand behind my head, slowly bringing my face closer to his. The coolness of his lips on mine is reassuring "Exactly," he says, catching me off guard.

I lift my head up and look down at him with raised eyebrows. "What...what are you talking about?" I ask, bewildered.

"The way I see it, if your faith is so strong then you shouldn't be doubting it. Just drink the milk. What's the big deal? You and I both know this is just some superstitious crap. Our baby is already growing inside you, sweetheart, so - just like you said a few seconds ago yourself - nothing will change anything."

I think long and hard about his words. He's right. I have faith. Strong faith. I know that no milk, dread-locked swami or boy-doll can change my baby's destiny.

Chapter Six
Tara!

Choudhary Niwas is once again a joyous place. There are two reasons why. First is that I've been a good, obedient daughter-in-law and have been gulping down half a stainless steel tumbler of the magic milk formula every morning at four a.m. for the last seven days.

But today I get to sleep in. No weird looking old, shrivelled Medicine Woman, shrouded in a charcoal-grey cloak, knocking on my door at a quarter to four, instructing me to change the will of nature in my belly. No swallowing some viscous, saadhu-blessed, white bachha-jhooth (milk from a cow which has given birth to a male off spring) liquid, mixed with ash-coloured M&M-sized pills.

Bi-ji is the happiest of all. She seems certain her Medicine Woman has not let her down (though cases have been reported of unsuccessful milk formula, so Didi tells me). Everyone else at home is simply pleased that the air is no longer fogged with an unbearable silence and occasional fearful whispers.

The second reason Choudhary Niwas has a happy-happy-joy-joy atmosphere is that it is now the season of festivals. Navratri, Dusshera, Karva Chauth, Diwali, Guru Nanak Jayanti, Ramadan, Eid. There is hustle and bustle in the bazaar and the exotic smells of food and sweetmeats wafting in the air makes me terribly homesick. Not because one feels the Indian festive season much in the western countries but because Ma always took extra efforts to celebrate her Hindu festivals with zest.

She used to make sure Pouja and I had the best ghagra-cholis, a long skirt with a cropped blouse and veil to match, to wear on each of these occasions. Ma spent hours and many dollars in Mount Roskill's and Papatoetoe's Indian shops, feeling the fabrics, matching the accessories and instructing the choli tailor about the latest neck designs she had chosen from Hindi movies. She would busy herself weeks in advance making mouth-watering sweetmeats - barfi, ghughra, kharkhariya, jalebi, laddoo, mohan-thaar, magaz - and she would buy small packets of powdered dyes and transform our front and back porches into a colourful canvas of intricate rangoli patterns, a ritual to welcome Goddess Lakshmi, the bringer of wealth and prosperity.

As the days pass my belly begins to show a teeny weeny bit. I keep whinging to Didi that it's not big enough and she keeps scolding me to enjoy its smallness now, for when it grows all big and heavy I'll be impatiently waiting to get the delivery over and done with. She also reminds me about Indian summers and how unbearably hot it will be during May, which is when the baby is due to arrive.

I look forward to the postman's visits, hoping to receive a letter from Ma. We haven't spoken since the last outburst.

"It's all my fault. Everything is always my fault. I should never have hurt Ma like that. She has every right to be upset with me," I vent my feelings to Didi.

"You got it off your chest and that's what's most important. And maybe Aunty Kavita also got a few things off hers." Didi's wrists grip the rolling pin as the golf-ball-sized dough gradually rolls outwards into a circular disk. "It'll all be fine in a couple of weeks. A mother and daughter can never have a permanent grudge. It may seem like there's a wall between the two that will never break but one day everything is forgotten and forgiven. You are a part of her…literally." Didi makes it sound so simple. She obviously doesn't know about the many Hollywood actresses who spend their lives hating their mothers.

As Didi had predicted, I receive a courier parcel from Ma. There is no sign of any hostility in the contents. She sends me the Karva Chauth shagun, together with a nice pair of jeans that have a stretchy pouch to cater for my expanding belly, and three turtleneck sweaters from my favourite Auckland shops. There are also three pastel coloured envelopes - pink, lilac and blue - each with a greeting card. One wishes me a Happy Diwali; the other two are Blue Mountain cards from Ma and Pouja.

Gurveer spends more time with me and less time going away on business trips with Papa-ji. Our little angel is creating a stronger bond between us. In the privacy of our bedroom we often think of prospective names for our bub. "Punjabi names…I like Punjabi names," I tell him.

"Why not Gujji?"

"Cos they're a bit boring. Punjabi names sound much more passionate."

"If you say so, Ms Patel," he teases secretly elated, I bet.

So far we've come up with some wonderful names, none too hard to pronounce. And we've decided to have the suffix Preet for a girl and Veer for a boy. Gurveer reckons the prefix doesn't have to be a pure Sikh name, it can be Gujrati as long as it goes nicely with the suffix. We'll just have to wait and see, I guess.

With winter becoming heavier each day, we spend most mornings sitting near the fire in the outside kitchen, warming our hands and feet over the burning pats of dried cow dung. Thanks to Ramu and Raju we have a whole stack of them piled up high near the earthen stove. Neighbours usually come to ask for them when they run out of firewood or their own cow dung patties. I always joke about putting up a sign, just above where the Choudhary Niwas sign is, that reads **COWS' MILK AND DRIED SHIT FOR SALE.**

*****

Gurveer is especially caring and concerned on Karva Chauth, the day I fast from dawn till moon rise for his health, prosperity and longevity. "Are you sure you wanna do this? You don't have to, you know," he tells me, his one arm wrapping my shoulders from behind and the other hand gently stroking my belly. "Why don't you miss this one and start from next year? Going without food and water might not be best for our bubba."

He may be right but I'm fervent enough to go through it, and I don't want to feel like a failure in front of Didi and Bi-ji. "I'll be fine," I reassure him.

This is my first Karva Chauth fast. Though I'm familiar with most Hindu festivals and rituals, thanks to Ma, Karva Chauth is something I have yet to experience or fully understand the significance of.

As a little girl I remember many Gujrati women observing this day-long, no-food, no-water (not even a drop) fast in Suva. One time I asked Ma why she wasn't doing the fast with all the other women in our little Gujji community. Ma had dismissed my curiosity with an abrupt, "Your Pappa is not worth it. He will be so busy screwing every gandi nangi girl that he'll forget to even turn up for the moonrise puja. Why should I go hungry and thirsty for a fuckwit like him?"

Even as an eight-year-old I could see the sense in that. Though this was the first and probably the last time

I saw my mother make the right decision when it came to the degree of submissiveness she shrouded herself within Pappa's presence or for that matter my grandmother's.

The fasting day drags ever so slowly. Thankfully the cold weather doesn't make me thirsty. In the past I have gone without food on Navratri fasts, but never without water. Today's fast makes me realise how important water is for our bodies. A little part of me feels guilty for keeping the fast as it means not being able to take my pregnancy supplements for my little one, but it's too late now to break the fast.

I look at my watch. Four o'clock. Four and half more hours before the moon is expected to rise. My last meal was last night's dinner. I ate it with little enthusiasm because my taste buds yearned for chicken curry, but every living being in Choudhary Niwas is vegetarian so I had to suppress my cravings.

Normally Gurveer wouldn't mind me having chicken or lamb or fish in New Zealand but here, he believes, we must respect his parents' wishes and I shouldn't eat any non-vegetarian dishes within these four walls.

Later in my room I hogged on a king size Mars bar that Ma sent in the parcel.

Didi and Bi-ji ate before sunrise this morning and drank chai and lassi. It's recommended that women eat well before sunrise to ensure they have enough energy to sustain throughout the day and evening, and sometimes most of the night when the moon decides not to rise until a little before midnight. Didi came to wake me up to participate in their pre-sunrise devour but I have never been a big eater in the morning and especially not at four a.m.

Their concern for my lack of energy proves legit as I begin complaining of a severe pain on my left temple two hours before moonrise. It's not so much the hunger that weakens me as the thirst. For a few seconds I close my eyes and give thanks to Goddess Lakshmi who blesses us with food and water, clothes and money, and all luxuries of life. So often I take the basic necessities for granted and yet somewhere deep in the desert of Rajasthan, where it hasn't rained for years, young children are dying of thirst everyday.

Gurveer massages my temples as I lie on his lap, my eyelids closed. I distract myself from the bhangra songs on the Alpha Punjabi TV channel in the periphery. This is one of the few times that Gurveer doesn't hold back from showing his affection for me in front of his family.

Like a birdsong, a sweet hum reaches my ears as Didi announces that the moon has risen and it's time for the puja to break the fast. Eight-thirty sharp, dead on time. Very few things are on time in India.

Taking the flat, brass puja thali plate that I had decorated in the morning, I join Didi and Bi-ji in our front entrance courtyard. We stand in a line with our heads covered by our duppatta veils. Opposite each of us stands our Pati Parmeshwar, God-like Husband, tall and important-looking. We place in front of our faces around channi, the sieve used for separating grainy particles from the smooth, velvety chappatti flour. A lit diya lamp rests on its metal rim.

We gaze at the moon through the minuscule gauze holes of the sieve, praying for our husband's long life, good health and prosperity, and immediately afterwards look at our husband's face. The path of our vision must not deviate, so that the moon's blessings are passed directly onto our husband.

Didi and Bi-ji perform these rituals with grace and perfection. The thalis and channis in their hands move swiftly and confidently while I struggle to keep up, my hands trembling. I look at the moon and say my prayers for Gurveer's wellbeing. At the same time a little critical part of me laughs at myself for standing with a sieve in front of a dead star. I wonder if there are any NASA guys up there. And if so what would their wives be doing right now? Reading a magazine perhaps? Watching *The Bold And The Beautiful* or *Oprah*? Lucky they took the American flag off otherwise it would be flapping down at me, each sweeping whoosh making a mockery of this sexist tradition. But that's just the Western me taking over. I'm sure there's an appropriate Vedic explanation to this practice or else it wouldn't have been followed with such loyalty for so many decades.

After bestowing a little water from a brass cup to Mother Earth, our husbands place the rim of the cup on our lips. We take the first sip to successfully break the fast. I notice Bi-ji touching Papa-ji's feet and Didi touching Pa-ji's. I follow suit.

Gurveer, being equally new to this, follows the trained actions of his fellow men and places both his palms flat on my bowed head to bless me with a long life of wifehood. "Sada suhagan raho," he whispers coyly, bestowing a blessing that very conveniently implies a longer lifespan for him. Not that I have anything against that.

Three years ago I'd have dismissed this ritual with a feminist sarcasm. Today I'm not only going hungry and thirsty for my husband's supposed long life, but also touching his feet for blessings as though he's some kind of deity! Why I'm going with the flow - fasting, drinking magic milk, covering my head, and suppressing my non-vegetarian cravings - I don't know. It's not like I feel forced to do any of them. Ultimately they have been my decisions.

Somehow it feels like I have always been this way. Always living and doing things for someone else.

*****

Whilst the entire city seems an epitome of celebrations, Tara remains quiet during her work hours. In our daily half-hour tuitions she makes an effort to be her old self but I can see she lives with the guilt of not telling the police about her husband.

She appears thinner and her chin is pointier now that all the fat has disappeared. She doesn't tie her hair in various styles anymore like she used to. Nowadays it's one ordinary plait which is sometimes untidy, as though she forgot to unplait it the night before and slept on it.

My daily routine question to her "Tara, you okay?" is always replied to with a weak smile and a nod and eventually a whisper, "Yes, Memsahib, okke okke."

I want to reach out to her but she has cocooned herself inside an unbreakable shell. It breaks my heart to see her deep in thought when she sits by the earthen stove in the outside kitchen, her hands sticky with chappatti dough.

Inside the house Didi, Bi-ji, Preetu and I might be watching TV or laughing and joking happily while poor Tara sticks to the employer-employee boundary that Bi-ji's stern looks always manage to imply.

With each passing day I feel guilty for putting Tara in this mute mode. Perhaps if I'd kept my big mouth shut and not told Tara off about her husband in my heat of the-moment insensitiveness, she would still be happy-go-lucky. How ignorant I can be sometimes of the undying commitment and faithfulness of these submissive Indian women. How stupid of me to think that my five-minute lecture to Tara about how her fucking paedophile husband deserves to be behind bars would change anything. You must apologise to her, I scold myself.

I decide to tell Tara how sorry I am to have lashed out at her that afternoon. And when she forgives me - which I hope she does - I will try and persuade her to seek help from Sanjana Singh.

It's almost twilight when I go looking for Tara, expecting that she'd still be helping in the kitchen, but Didi tells me she has left already. "Why, what's wrong? Need anything?" Didi asks.

"No, Didi, I'm fine, I just wanted to tell her something about tomorrow's tuition," I lie. As much as it would be a load off my chest to share the truth with Didi I must honour the trust Tara has bestowed upon me.

I wish Tammy were here right now. She doesn't know Tara and so telling her would be safe. I sleep restlessly, battling with the unfairness of the world. Realising I have so much to be happy about while Tara has so much to be sad about.

It's a relief to see the sun radiating through the mulish clouds the next morning. As winter sets in the sun plays hide and seek behind these grey curtains for most of the day, and it often becomes hard to dry the washing. For the past couple of days I've been opting to wear my tracksuits rather than salwaar kameezes. Someone once told me it never gets very cold in India and now I feel like thumping that someone's head with Didi's rolling pin.

Winter in Punjab is the worst I have ever experienced. Auckland gets cold but Punjab's winter is much worse. The horrid thing about Choudhary Niwas is it has marble floors. It's perfect during summer to lie on the floor and relax from the coolness of the smooth, flat tile slabs. But in winter, boy oh boy, the house feels like a chilly bin.

The warmth of the morning sun refreshes me as I do my gentle hatha sun salutations and deep breathing on the terrace roof. I keep my eyes focussed on the front gate, hoping to see Tara coming in, perhaps in a happier mood this morning. It's probably best for me to say sorry to her this early so she can have a better day. I must tell her that I'm still her friend and that I'll help in any which way I can to get her and her children past this trauma.

Seven o'clock comes and goes and there is no sign of Tara.

Breakfast and lunch time come and go, and still no sign of Tara.

"Wanna join me for a nap?" Gurveer asks, rubbing his pot belly as though he is the one carrying our little bubba.

With so many leftovers from Diwali, the festival of lights, two days ago we've been stuffing ourselves with the plethora of curries and parathas and sweets. No wonder we both find it so hard to climb the last couple of steps to our bedroom.

I'm about to switch the heater on when Didi's shrilling screams startle me and cause the power cord to fall from the socket where I had half fitted it in.

Gurveer throws off the razai and dashes outside to find out what the matter is. Placing my duppatta back on my shoulders, I follow Gurveer down the steps, carefully descending each one.

"Tara, hai rubba, Tara, rubba o rubba, Tara...." cries Didi.

Tara is nowhere in sight, yet Didi is in a hysterical state.

"Bhabi-ji, ki hoya, dusso bhi." Gurveer begs to tell him what is going on.

"Le gaye Tara nu chak ke police wale," Didi wails. *The police took her.*

"Good!" I blurt out, giving loud claps. Finally my dear Tara has come to her senses and told the police about her husband. Then I try to hide my relief, suddenly remembering Tara's promise. Didi glares at me. "What do you mean, good, Priya?" she asks.

I may as well tell them that I've known all along and that they should support Tara's decision to tell the police instead of feeling sorry for that bastard husband of hers. "It's about bloody time she got that sick bastard arrested after what he did."

Gurveer and Didi stare at me, Gurveer's face even more blank with confusion than Didi's. "Priya...no, that's not it," says Didi, regaining her composure. "It's not her husband who is arrested. It's Tara! Her husband's in hospital fighting for his life. The police took Tara this morning. Everyone's talking about it. She's done something awful to him...hai rubba, how to tell you?" She cries hysterically again.

What? How can that be? Surely, there's been a mistake. "They've got it all wrong. Tara didn't do anything - he's the one. How come they arrested her?" I scream with anger and confusion.

Didi places her cupped palms over her mouth as though ashamed of what her mouth wants to say. She gives a cautious glance to see if maybe Papa-ji is around, but he is nowhere in sight so she says, "Tara cut off her husband's manhood."

Gurveer's face turns deathly pale as his hands

move to comfort his own crotch but stop midway, perhaps because he's remembered his sister-in-law's presence next to him.

Nothing had prepared me for this shocking news. It's all my fault. I told her that if I were in her place I'd cut the bastard's dick off. And she's done exactly that.

I hug Didi tightly and let out a painful cry, shaking horribly. Gurveer and Didi console me, thinking that it's the news of losing Tara that hurts me because I'd grown close to her. They are partly right, but mostly I'm crying for my unspoken apology. Maybe if I had apologised to Tara sooner, this day would never have come and I would not have lost my only friend in this country.

Later that evening I find out, and so does everyone else, that Tara's husband had tried to rape Meenaxi the previous night. It was all too much for Tara to handle, so she cut off the root of the problem. No dick. No rape. No problem.

As details of Tara's inflictions sink in, I coax myself that it's not my fault after all. That Tara is indeed a woman of substance. That there comes a time in a woman's life when dictations of traditions cease to mean much because her virtue and identity are being threatened. That Tara did what any woman in her place would have done. That she is a hero. A twenty-first century Jhansi ki Rani.

My heart fills with elation as I sit up straight and tall, and most of all proud of my dear friend whom I may never see again. I close my eyes and focus on the forces of telepathy, something I once learnt in a metaphysics workshop. Saying them just as Tammy would, I whisper these words and hope Tara can hear me, wherever she is right this moment: "You go, girlfriend!"

Chapter Seven
Stepping the Boundary

Gurveer has a Thursday fetish. "Pira da din honda hei," he tells me. He is a staunch Pir devotee, an aspect of Sufism, and visits the Baba Shaakhu Pir Temple every Thursday evening. As a young boy Gurveer would buy the little plastic packet of mustard oil sold outside the temple and light a lamp to pray for his exams and to be a good person. "Whenever something nice happens to me I notice it's a Thursday," he often says.

Most times he's right. We had our first lunch date on a Thursday, had our first kiss on a Thursday and, being a girlie-girl who remembers all important dates and events in my love life and otherwise, I know we first made love on a Thursday. He was born on a Thursday and so was I. We got married on a Thursday. See, so far, all good.

Today is another ordinary Thursday, with the December winter fog beginning to lift its depressing shroud. Amidst Bi-ji's ear-deafening snores and Didi's growls at Rannu and Preetu to stop eating so much jalebi or else they will have "bund vich keedhia" - a bum full of worms - Gurveer and I struggle to listen to the CNN news on TV.

Images of the gigantic, decorated Christmas tree in New York's Rockfella makes my eyes moist as I remember my favourite Christmas moment: Hyde Park's carols by candlelight, which I religiously attended every year. This year has gone a lot quicker, but then it seems this way every year. I once heard that somebody has actually proved that the world's speed increases everyday!

"Do you think I should ring the Immigration people in Delhi to find out what's happening with your

visa application?" I ask Gurveer, realising it has been
almost a year since we lodged for his New Zealand
residency visa. Ma is right, sometimes we need to, as the
famous Indian saying goes, twist our finger to get the
ghee out of the bottle if it doesn't come out with a
straight one.

Gurveer takes the TV remote from his mouth,
which he had been chewing onto, and places it on the
coffee table. Flipping through the tabletop calendar he
counts out loud the number of months that have passed
since he had his Immigration Health Check. "Bloody
hell, it's been four months already! What are these guys
doing, man? Yeah, let's call. Do you wanna do it or
should I?"

"I think it's better if I call because I'm a Kiwi
citizen, and also I can tell them that we're pregnant and
want to deliver our baby in New Zealand. Maybe they'll
hurry things up that way. After all, it's not like we're
lying to them about being pregnant, I mean. We can fax
them Dr Siddhu's letter if they want to see proof," I tell
him, trying to sound convincing.

After several attempts at a dubious apparatus that
Papa-ji calls a phone I finally manage to get through to
the New Delhi phone number appearing on Gurveer's
immigration documents. A few minutes later I'm
transferred from the automated voice welcoming me to
the New Zealand Consulate, and passed on to a real
person. She greets me politely with a convent-educated
accent and requests Gurveer's application details. I hear
the tapping on her keyboard as she confirms my
identification and asks me to hold while she reads about
the progress of the application.

"Apologies, ma'am, your husband's application has
taken a little longer than expected. We've had thousands of

applications, and though we say nine to twelve months sometimes things need to be verified," the woman explains after reading the file notes on her computer.

Just as I'm about to give her an earful about my New Zealand rights and how I'm pregnant and how the system sucks and how I'm seriously craving some great tasting café latte which I can only get in Ponsonby not Punjab, she continues in a tone so pleasant I can almost hear her smile, "Nevertheless, Ms Patel, I am pleased to inform you that a letter has been put in the mail for Mr Gurveer Choudhary only this morning granting him his provisional residency. You should have it in the next couple of days. All the necessary details are in the letter. He will need to either come in himself or send us his passport so we can place a visa sticker on it. Is there anything else I can help you with today, Ms Patel?"

I want to hug this woman and tell her she's the best customer service person in India. It is a great feeling to be told what I really want to hear without having to pay a single bribing rupee.

"Oh, thank you, thank you, thank you. You've been great. I really appreciate all your help," I chatter on, sounding like a happy lunatic high on some drug.

Two days later, just as the lady had told me, the letter arrives in the mail confirming Gurveer's residency permit. The postman guesses that we are anticipating good news and hassles us to give him a "party" before he will hand us the envelope. He really means "Give me a hundred rupees or thereabouts to celebrate your good fortune." Not one for giving bribes, this time I relent and tip him one hundred and one rupees for good luck. This news is exhilarating and deserves celebration.

Here in India, from what I've noticed, bribery exists in religion as much as it exists among human folk.

When one wants an ideal husband, a dream job, a pay rise, a son, or fulfilment of any other materialistic wishes, one promises to bestow to the God idols sweets, coconuts, even gold. Sometimes when one is a little practical food for the poor is promised.

Bi-ji's promise to Guru Nanak Dev Ji was that when Gurveer got his visa we would all pay a visit to the Golden Temple in Amritsar, the largest and most renowned Gurdwara in Sikhism. Very early the next morning we pile into a hired eight seater Toyota Qualis four-wheel drive taxi. The driver, a shy, thin young man whose pretty boy face is fair like the colour of chickpea flour, graciously accepts a gazillion rupees from Papa-ji and promises a smooth car ride.

From my little panicky sighs each time we pass a pot hole the driver obviously senses that I'm pregnant or unwell, or maybe just a whinging NRI. A journey that normally takes about three hours takes us five, but nobody is complaining. Rannu and Preetu sleep most of the way, Rannu's head on Didi's lap and Preetu's on mine. Their excitement at going to see the Golden Temple for the first time had kept them awake most of the night last night, and now with the tortoise-speed Qualis and the warm motherly laps, the little angels barely let several minutes pass by before beginning their soft snores.

Inside the Golden Temple I am mesmerised. The only word I can use to describe how I feel standing inside this majestic monument to God and truth is peace. This is the first time I feel truly at peace with myself, with the system in this country and with the injustices that have shrouded my world ever since I swam in Ma's belly.

The sweet sound of prayer kirtan echoes amidst the imposing buildings capped with pure gold foil. The morning sun reflects into the lake on which this shrine sits, like millions of little diamond clusters and the sweet scent of fresh halwa prashaad dangles in the air.

All around me is a sea of people with colourful duppatta or turban covered heads. People who, like Bi-ji, have come for muthha tek, the physical act of touching one's forehead to the temple floors as a result of a wish coming true. Some come to experience the beauty of this Sikh temple and some live here to serve God. Opportunities exist for visitors to do their sewa, a voluntary service where one can help in the kitchen with vegetable peeling or rolling out chapattis, or washing dirty dishes after they come back from the langar room where meals are served.

Ma has taken Pouja and me to just about every Hindu temple in Suva and Auckland. Gurveer took me to a Gurdwara for the first time three days after we'd confessed our love for each other. The Otahuhu Gurdwara in Auckland holds a special place in the memory chamber of my heart. There I had my first Sikh experience, which made me look forward to living in Punjab even more.

The best thing about Sikh temples is that there are no beggars inside the temples, maybe outside but never inside. Since most beggars in India beg to fill their empty stomachs, Sikh temples make sure there is plenty to eat for all visitors, caste and religion no bar. By contrast, many Hindu temples in India buzz with beggars outside and inside, and Hindu priests are no less when it comes to hassling. They can smell a foreigner from a distance and will demand astronomical amounts to place at the feet of marble deity statues. Sadly, most gullible foreigners give in to this profit-making gimmick and end up being taken for a ride.

I'm surprised to find a girl, probably around my age, less if anything, outside the Golden Temple gates. She tugs at my duppatta and says, "Bibbi ji, ek paisa de do, dekhna Bhagwaan tumko beta dega," begging me to give her some money and promising that in return God will give me a son. I can see she has a little belly herself, maybe five or six months.

Bi-ji gives her the kind of look she often gave Tara whenever Tara wasn't looking, but only meaner. "Chee chee, ja koi kaam koom kar le, chalo hatto!" Go find a job and clear off. "These good for nothing girls - when will they learn that begging is a sin? See, she's pregnant too! Chee chee chee, so dirty, no sign of who the father of this munhoos child would be."

Like Tara, this girl has some sort of energy that makes me smile at her. She takes my smile as a green sign for money and hops across the road to me, her belly swaying from side to side and up and down beneath her torn purple duppatta. She has a silver ring on her nose, and her teeth and lips are stained with betel juice.

"De do nah, Bibbi-ji," she begs.

"Yeh lo," I say, giving her a ten rupee note, which she accepts by kissing the note like a mother greeting her long lost child.

As the Choudhary party climbs back into the taxi for the return journey, I look out the window and see the girl happily bouncing across the road towards another young foreigner woman for some paisa.

As usual she accepts some coins from this generous lady and gives her a blessing for a son. The same blessing she gave me, the same blessing I've been receiving since the day I got married - the same blessing every new bride of India receives.

Obviously those who give this blessing fail to realise the consequences of wishing their nation to be filled with sons. I keep listening to our mohalla women complaining about not being able to find any girls to marry their sons off to. I'm always tempted to shake them and yell back, "There can only be enough girls around to marry your sons if you stupid women allow girls to be born!"

As our Qualis honks through the narrow alleyways infested with tongas, horses, cattle, people and dirt, I fix my eyes on the beggar girl until her image becomes lost in the cloud of dust particles that rise with each revolution of the taxi's tyres. I say a silent prayer for her, similar to the one I said for my own baby when I was inside the temple. Satnaam Wahe Guru, bless her child with good health, wisdom and compassion.

******

*Friday 27*ʰ *December, 2002*

My darling tummy bubba,

You are twenty weeks old and I'm starting to feel your kicks now. Sometimes you are like a little gymnastics pro, turning somersaults every few minutes. I find that you like to rest during the day and become playful at nights. My sweet, sweet bubba, your papa and I can't wait to hold you in our arms.

Rest well, my darling. Mumma loves you, forever.

I paste the latest computer image photo of my twenty weeks ultrasound onto the opposite page of the journal entry. My little one is blessed to have a photo whilst still inside my belly.

"All is fine and okay. BP normal, baby's heartbeat normal and Mrs Choudhary, you are a good girl, your weight gain is very very good. Keep doing what you are doing and no need to worry about anything. Call me if you have any questions," Dr Siddhu had told me during yesterday's check up and ultrasound.

So why does he want to see me again tomorrow?

Dr Siddhu's phone call last night had scared me. Bi-ji had been on the phone to him before she had handed me the receiver, cheerfully exchanging her pleasantries with "Daaktar Saab". She smiled gleefully as I put the phone to my ear.

I greeted the doctor pleasantly, trying not to sound alarmed."Is everything okay, Doctor-Ji? I thought you said our baby is fine."

"Sure, sure, nothing like that," he announced. "Just come in tomorrow for an amniocentesis."

Amnio…what? Though I'm fairly confident our baby is healthy and growing well, medical procedures and Dr Siddhu's jargons always make me nervous.

He explained the procedure, saying he was going to inject a needle into the embryo and take some amniotic fluid from it. "It's a routine check for any genetic disorders. You see, you have waited too long to have a child - you're what, twenty-eight almost twenty-nine years now, nah? That's why only, we must do this test. It's required. No need to worry. Tell your husband I have fixed your appointment for eleven tomorrow morning."

With that he hung up briskly.

I wasn't getting a good feeling about this. Why was it so necessary to start poking inside my bubba's comfortable warm home? And what did he mean, twenty-nine is too old to have a baby? I'd read about healthy pregnancies for women who were forty plus!

*****

Gurveer's head rests at the crook of my neck, his soft snores tickling my skin. I lie awake. This time it's not because of bubba's kicks but because I'm not convinced I really need to go through this am-neurotic thing.

A pregnant woman's instincts are never wrong. I must read more about this thing before I let him prod into my tummy. Luckily I find the December issue of *Parenting* sitting in the pile of magazines on my bedside table. I pray for some kind of literature to pop up at me about this procedure in these glossy pictures, with the world's cutest angels on them.

Bingo! A little blurb on amniocentesis confirms what Dr Siddhu told me - it's nothing but a scan to detect genetic abnormalities. Good, now I can sleep. Oh, but wait, it says it's normally only for women over thirty five. My shoulders begin to tense.

Sleep doesn't come easily, and when I finally doze off I find myself bathing in the lake at the Golden Temple - calm and tranquil at first, but then I begin to swim faster and faster, trying to escape from a giant needle lurking behind me like a hungry shark.

*****

Gurveer holds onto my fidgety hands as we drive in our family car. We leave half an hour early for Dr Siddhu's Clinic so we don't have to speed.

As we approach the area where Dr Siddhu's clinic is, Gurveer lets out a frustrated cry. A single file of cars is blocking the lane entrance. Driving a little further in, we realise they are all police vehicles.

Having no other choice, we park our car in someone's driveway and walk the few extra blocks to get to the clinic. "What's all this?" Gurveer asks the security officer who always stands at the clinic gates to let people in and out.

Before the officer can answer two police officers approach us in their khaki uniforms and demand to see some identification.

"What for?" Gurveer asks with impatience and haste in his tone, and a little agitation that only I can detect.

"Just do as I say. No one is allowed in here, okay? Who are you and why are you here?" one of the officers demands, his face serious.

Gurveer pulls out his leather Guess wallet that I gave him on Valentine's Day last year and shows the police officers his New Zealand driver's licence. One officer squints at the plastic card as though Gurveer has just provided him counterfeit rupee notes. The other reads the name and immediately flashes his tartar coated teeth. "Very sorry, Choudhary Sarji. Don't mind, please. I didn't recognise you after all these years. Your father and Jasveer Sarji I see all the time, but you, Sarji, I hear went to phoren." The tartar teeth flash again while the doubtful officer joins in with little nods and head shakes and an equally wide smile.

"That's fine, officer," says Gurveer. "What's the problem anyway? My wife has an appointment for eleven a.m. Is Dr Siddhu available?"

The two officers look at each and swallow simultaneously. Officer Doubtful is about to speak when Officer Happy stops him and nods. He appears to be the senior one. "Sar-ji, Dr Siddhu is in very very big trouble."

"Trouble? How do you mean?" Gurveer asks.

"Sarji, early today morning somebody found remains of aborted foetus in a rubbish dump a few metres from the clinic. We also have a witness who says she saw a nurse from this clinic putting the plastic bag in the dump last night. Sarji, it turns out this is a serious case of female foeticide."

"You're joking, right?" a perplexed Gurveer asks.

"Not joking, Sarji. By now the police must have also found out the family who is responsible for this. More and more of these murders are happening, and sadly our Punjab seems to be the worst offending state. Some cases get reported, some don't. Luckily this time the witness is a school teacher and loves children. So now Hoshiarpur police have taken Dr Siddhu for questioning and that nurse too. If what people are saying about Dr Siddhu, that he kills unborn girl babies for thousands of rupees, is true then he will definitely be arrested and charged. Sorry, Sar-ji, looks like you and Madam-ji will have to find a new doctor."

My ears are throbbing with pain and I'm barely able to comprehend what the officer is saying. Gurveer stares at him, his mouth half open in horror.

"Oh my God!" I manage to say, realising these are my first words to these officers.

Gurveer looks at me and shakes his head, knowing well that after listening to the officer's story I could do just about any act of crime. He places an arm around my shoulders and motions me towards our car. "Thanks, Officer," he says to the policeman.

I remain quiet in the car, too numbed from shock to speak. It doesn't bother me that I have to find a new doctor. What bothers me is how I'm supposed to find one I can trust who hasn't been committing acts of murder.

Two years ago when Emma, one of my work acquaintances in Auckland, had an abortion I couldn't find any compassion or empathy for her while everyone else at work treated her as if she'd done a Nobel-Prize winning deed. Her excuse was that she couldn't afford to have another baby because her boyfriend gambled all their money in poker machines. That, to me, was a lame excuse for not being responsible of her actions. Where was her wisdom when she had her stiletto heeled legs hanging in the air for him?

As the years passed I realised that abortion in New Zealand was common. Most women had them because of teenage pregnancies, some because they had "accidents", some because they didn't want to bring a child into an abusive relationship. But at least they never had them because they didn't want a girl baby.

Welcome to the son-obsessed nation of India, Priya. To murder a child because she is a girl! And while she's still floating in the comfort of her mother's womb temporarily protected from the atrocities that await her if she was allowed to live.

I cry in the car all the way home, with Gurveer letting out little gasps of hopelessness for his country. He pulls over at Five Bells cafeteria on Session Chowk and hugs me tight, my growing belly sandwiched between us as though in a group hug. My soft cries turn into uncontrollable sobs. "I can't deal with this anymore, Jaanu! What's the use of bathing in the Ganges? Why do they pray to Ma Durga, Ma Lakshmi? They are all female idols! Why don't they realise this? Such hypocritical bastards this country is filled with." I sob into Gurveer's chest, my kohl eyeliner smudging on his beige sweater.

"Ssh, don't cry, meri jaan. I'm so sorry about all this, Priya," he whispers into my hair. We let several seconds pass before pulling apart from each other.

It's as though Gurveer had been reading my mind. He cups his hands around my messy cheeks and says, "Let's go back to Auckland. I've got my visa, so it's not like we need approval from anyone to do what feels right for us."

As much as he's right and it's probably the best thing for us to go back to New Zealand, I want Gurveer's family to be a part of the celebrations when I deliver our baby. And for that we'd have to have the baby here.

I can almost feel the nerve synapses in my brain toying with the pros and cons of going back to a country which was never quite the home that India has become or that Fiji was once.

*****

Bi-ji opens the gate to let the car in. She doesn't look too well; her eyes are swollen and red. Had she been crying, I wonder.

It turns out she has been. Usually she's excited every time I come back from my check-ups and welcomes me with much pampering and enthusiasm. It's nothing like that today.

"Ki hoya, Bi-ji, sab theek to hei?" Are you okay?" Gurveer asks her.

She takes the end of her olive-green kashmiri shawl and dabs at her eyelids with it. "Just some really bad news, pooth. Seebo and her whole family were arrested by police half an hour ago. Raju went to deliver them milk and saw the police taking them away."

Gurveer squints his eyes into focus, his mid-eyebrow skin folding into a pair of square brackets. He asks, "What for? What did they do?"

"Hai rubba, Seebo is such a good woman, always coming to satsang. So much she manages by herself after Lalit bhaisaab's death - the house, the big business, three sons and three bahus. Only problem is she only has one grandson and already four granddaughters. So when she told me her middle bahu was pregnant again I told her to go see Priya's doctor, maybe he can help. I hear he only takes five thousand rupees to fix everything. With Seebo's middle bahu the milk formula never works!"

I look at Gurveer in utter horror and grab the marble pillar tightly, feeling faint. Gurveer shakes his head rapidly in confusion. "Bi-ji, you sent Seebo Maasi to Dr Siddhu...*you* sent her?" he asks shocked.

"Toh haur ki kardi mein?" Bi-ji challenges. *What else was there to do?*

"Bi-ji, do you know that Dr Siddhu has been arrested?"

"I know, I know, that's what I can't understand. I mean, everybody goes to him for this sort of thing but it's bechaari Seebo's ill-fate that when she goes all this mess has to happen. Before that, when Banso, Jagindro and Satya went to Daaktar saab for their bahus, nothing like this ever happened...poor bechaari Seebo."

"Bi-ji, don't you get it? Have you gone nuts or something?" Gurveer lashes out. "They killed the unborn baby because it was a girl. Seebo Maasi should have known it's illegal to pay a doctor to kill a girl foetus."

Bi-ji snaps, "Uff, what illegal villegal! It happens here all the time. You've been away far too long from your soil and now you come back talking like a phirengi. Pooth, Seebo only did what's right."

I want to take Bi-ji's duppatta and strangle her with it. All the love and respect I've ever felt for her is seeping out of my pores in a cold sweat, and a pang of suspicion rises in my throat as I recall her chirpy manner on the phone to Dr Siddhu. What if she'd been planning the same deal for me?

Things begin to make more sense now. If I really needed an amniocentesis why didn't Dr Siddhu tell us about it two days ago when we had the detailed scan? Why on the phone? And I never really heard the phone ring that time either. Perhaps it was Bi-ji who called him instead of the other way around. And *Parenting* magazine said a woman needs to be over thirty-five before the test is necessary. If Bi-ji can suggest something so sinful to her friends, surely she feels the same malice for my baby?

Without thinking, I unleash my venom and attack my mother-in-law like never before, not even on the night of the milk-formula fight. "You murderer! You organised today's appointment, didn't you? You wanted to do the same to me like what this fucking Seebo woman did to her bahu," I scream.

"Priya, don't be ridiculous!" Gurveer yells back, his mood suddenly in favour of his murderous mother. "You don't know what you're saying. Bi-ji had nothing to do with our appointment!"

Bi-ji purses her lips together and scowls. Her deep heavy sighs sound like a pressure cooker about to blow its whistle. "I knew this would happen one day," she grunts. "You phoren girls with your mouths moving like sharp sharp scissors. Hai rubba, all I did was talk to Seebo and make a suggestion. How dare you accuse me of any of this!"

She picks herself from her squatting position and marches off to her room. A loud bang follows as she shuts the wooden doors.

"I'm leaving. Are you coming or not?" I ask Gurveer, who looks at me like he has seen a ghost.

"What do you mean leaving? Why?" he dares to ask.

"Because I can't live with murderers, that's fucking why!"

"Why do you always have to overreact, Priya?"

"Overreact? You heard her. She helped kill that

baby. Can't you see what she's capable of? Don't pretend like you don't know. Ever since I came into this house there's so much pressure to have a son. She even has the fucking decency to arrange for some lousy milk, like that's going to give her a grandson. Now she's trying to murder my baby, and you're saying I'm overreacting! To hell with you and this place. I'm not going to put myself and my baby through this crap, no fucking way." I choke on the tears stuck in my throat.

"I don't know what to think anymore. You do whatever you want and so will I," retaliates Gurveer, throwing his Reebok cap across the porch like a Frisbee.

"Fine!"

"Fine!"

I storm up the stairs into my room to sort out what I need to do. Downstairs, I hear the Kinetic scooter roaring off into the distance

I can't stand this house anymore. I have to leave. Now. Until I know what I really want from my life - and my marriage for that matter - I will stay a few days in the Maharaja Hotel, some ten minutes' drive from Choudhary Niwas.

*****

In my small cabin bag I pack toiletries, underwear, flannelette pyjamas, my bumblebee journal and three pairs of salwaar kameezes. I check to see if I have enough money and my passport. Yes, I do. At least I have my New Zealand ATM card tucked safely in my Esprit wallet for any emergencies. I slide my wallet into my Saachi handbag, and with my cabin bag strap over my other shoulder I prepare to leave our bedroom.

One last look around the room fills me with resentment. I'm overcome by memories of the intimate moments Gurveer and I have shared within these pastel-blue walls. An uneasiness creeps into me, each step becoming heavier as though my feet are tied to a sack of soaked wool. One half of my heart says, *Priya, don't be a fool. This is your real home no matter what comes your way.* The determined chambers of my heart tell me otherwise.

The best thing that has happened in this room is our baby. And no mother-fucking doctor or mother-in-law will take that baby away from me. Girl or boy!

Downstairs, Didi's eyes are bloodshot. She knows this time that push has come to shove and there is no turning back for me.

"Don't say it, please Didi, I have to do this," I beg when I see her lips quivering with murmurs I refuse to listen to, in case they change my mind.

She nods and says, "No, you're right, sis, I won't stop you no matter how much I want to. Your courage will make up for all my weaknesses. I'll miss you, Priya."

Didi weeps in my arms. I assure her I'll be fine. After all, it's not like I'm moving very far. She can always hop in a rickshaw and come and see me. I promise to call her as soon as I've checked into the hotel.

She summons Raju to get me a taxi, quick. The Choudhary men aren't around so there's no male chauvinist pig to remind me about my vows of being a sati-savitri wife - one who must burn to death on her husband's funeral pyre, who must withstand every single evil deed that is bestowed upon her and never dare to cross the Lakshman-Rekha that defines the boundaries of a married woman.

*****

The phone rings several times in my hotel room. Each time I lift the receiver to say hello there is a long silence on the other end, and then a disconnecting click.

I suspect it's Gurveer. Didi must have given him the hotel room number. It's not her fault - she did ask me earlier if she could give my number to Gurveer and I only remained silent. My heart really wishes it's Gurveer missing me and calling. It wishes for him to knock on my door and tell me how sorry he is for not standing up for me.

Something tells me he knows I've done the right thing but his ego gets in the way when he wants to say the words on the phone. Then again, I could be wrong. It could just be a wrong number. I doubt it though.

I spend most of the night trying not to think about what happened earlier today. The TV programmes give me temporary anchor as I drown myself in the rapid images flicking at me from the Sony box. My mind switches back and forth between today's incidents and the colourful images on the screen. The fragrance of washing powder on the crisp laundered cotton sheets provides a welcome warmth.

Outside my room I can hear a baraat procession being greeted at the hotel's Marriage Hall entrance. Maybe that's why it's taking the room service guys two hours to get me a lousy cup of chai - they're probably too busy serving hot food to the dowry-hungry groom's party.

I really miss Didi's cooking. Even my little one notices the change of environment. There has been very few movements in my belly since I checked in to this awfully lonely but immaculately arranged deluxe room.

I had asked for a single room, but when the receptionist saw my red eyes and my one hand rubbing my belly while the other clutching onto my luggage she must have thought I was a lunatic NRI running away from my evil husband, and that I'd have plenty of foreign currency on me. I clearly told her this was only going to be for a couple of nights but she insisted I take the deluxe room at no extra charge. "Madam-ji, in your situation you need all the rest you can get and only our deluxe suite can offer you that. Don't worry, no extra charge okay? Compliments from the hotel," she'd insisted.

A deluxe room it is indeed! The walls are embellished with intricately encrypted Rajasthani artwork and the curtains are thick Thai silk and drop all the way down to the floor with flowing sari-like pleats. Limca and Coke bottles are neatly stacked in the mini bar, and on top of the fridge lies a basket of Parle-G chocolates and biscuits. The bathroom, my sanctuary in every hotel room I ever stay at, has a golden hue reflected from the ceiling spotlights. It has an enormous bath, three fluffy white towels of different lengths hanging on the steel rail, and an onyx marble vanity unit with little plastic bottles of liquid soap, shampoo and conditioner. A brass box of facial tissues and a vase of fresh flowers stand neatly tucked in each corner. Shiny golden knobs on the taps emit reflections of the posh surroundings.

On any other day I'd enjoy this luxury like a child in Disneyland, probably take countless baths and eat most of the confectionery. I'd snuggle up in the king sized bed using Gurveer's warm chest - which has just the right amount of hair - as my pillow and watch a classic Hindi movie on Zee Gold, after we'd made passionate love. On any other day.

The wee hours of the morning is when my eyelids decide to willingly join together. My first night in four years I sleep alone. Somehow I fall deep into sleep.

"Uff yaar," I curse, wishing the phone would stop

ringing this early in the morning. Who would be calling me at this hour?

My Pulsar wristwatch jolts me to reality. It's past ten a.m. *And no, Priya, it's not the phone that's buzzing, it's the doorbell. So get off your pregnant arse and open the door, or at least yell out to let the person know you are alive and well!*

"Didi!" I cry, flinging my arms around her as soon as I see her smiling face waiting patiently at the door.

Behind Didi is another woman who gives me a weak smile. She appears thin, almost waiflike. Her head reaches a little lower than mine and she wears a maroon salwaar kameez with a beige woollen cardigan. Her waist length hair is braided, with a black rubber band holding it in place. Her face looks familiar, but I'm not too sure who she reminds me of exactly. Perhaps a combination of two or three faces I know.

"Priya, this is Balwinder," Didi eventually says, placing her arm around the stranger.

Aha, now I see the resemblance - Bi-ji's eyes, Papa-ji's jaws, and the same shyness that I once saw in Gurveer when he asked me for my phone number.

Balwinder walks towards me reluctantly. She glances at Didi as though for approval to move closer to me. I immediately realise that she must feel uncomfortable meeting me for the first time since I'm a foreigner. I stretch my arms forward and hug her. "It's so nice to meet you finally, Bhabi," whispers Balwinder in between soft sobs.

"Oh, I can't tell you how much I've wanted to meet you," I reply, with tears rolling down my cheeks too.

Like long lost friends, we embrace for several minutes, pulling away every now and then to let

Balwinder cup her hands around my cheeks or kiss my forehead or rub my belly, and re-embrace me, affirming our forbidden sisterhood to each other.

After a quick shower I pick up the phone to dial the room service number for something sumptuous for breakfast. It dawns on me that it's been years since I last had a girlie brunch. I suddenly miss my home that lies across oceans.

"Don't bother, I've brought you these," Didi tells me, showing me a paper bag that has translucent oil stains on it, and a vacuum flask.

As we devour Didi's delicious methi parathas with mango achaar and sweet plain lassi, Didi breaks the silence and explains the reason for Balwinder's visit.

It turns out that Balwinder's mother-in-law has accused her of being a baanjh, a barren, unable to bear any children, and forced her out of the house, allowing her only to take her clothing and that was it. The mother-in-law had proudly announced to Balwinder that she'd found a younger, fertile girl for her son and so there was no need for Balwinder in the house anymore, unless she wanted to remain there as a maid!

Balwinder remains quiet, nodding occasionally as Didi relates the ill-fated events. With nowhere else to go, and no tertiary education or experience to get her a job, Balwinder had returned to her parents' home for support.

"What did Bi-ji and Papa-ji say?" I ask.

Didi looks at Balwinder, whose silent sobs turn into loud sniffles.

"They told her to go back to her husband. That she belongs in that house and it is her bad karma that she cannot produce an heir for her husband's family and so she must learn to accept her fate."

"What the fu--," I bite my tongue, reminding myself that I've been swearing a lot in the past couple of days and it's no good for my little one, who will have been listening to everything from inside my womb.

Monitoring my internal dialogue, I place my hand on Balwinder's shoulder reassuringly and say, "We can't let that happen now, can we?"

"But what else can I do, Bhabi?" asks Balwinder, her voice trembling with fear and hopelessness. "Where else do I go? I'd be better off dead than to have a kismat like mine," she continues, blaming her bad karma for her situation.

"How do you know you can't have a baby? Have you had a fertility test done that tells you that you can't have kids? What if it's your husband who's got the problem, huh? Then what? Your stupid mother-in-law can't fix the problem if it's her golden boy who's shooting blanks!"

Didi and Balwinder stare at me with uncomprehending faces as if I'm suddenly speaking Russian or some other foreign tongue they've never heard before.

It's Didi who dares to speak first. "Priya, is that possible?" she asks.

"What?" I ask.

"That it may not be Bal's fault, that maybe Birender is the one who has the problem? I mean, I saw a documentary on Doordarshan once about such things but I thought it was just another scientific myth...you know, like UFOs and all."

It's my turn to stare back as if they're a couple of retards. But this is no time for scrutiny, I remind myself. I have to move fast and give these gullible women a taste of what science is all about and make them realise how much they shroud themselves in old wives' tales. Specifically Punjabi old wives' tales!

I can think of only one person to call for advice. If this was Auckland there'd be no problem, but I can't be so confident that anyone else in this male dominated city will help Balwinder. However I know Sanjana Singh can.

Pulling Sanjana's business card out of my wallet, I request the hotel operator to connect me to Sanjana's mobile.

"So great to hear your voice, Priya," squeals Sanjana after we exchange our hellos.

"Yours too, Sanjana," I squeal back. "I'm sorry to call you like this but we need your help."

"We?"

"Me and Paramjeet Didi."

"Are you girls all right? What's the matter?"

I tell her Balwinder's story, and after listening attentively Sanjana takes a deep breath in. "Got a pen?" she asks, her voice composed and professional.

"Yup." I signal to Didi to pass me the pen lying next to the room service menu card on the glass table top.

"Great. Give me a second and I'll just find the names of people who can sort this mess out for you ladies. And tell Balwinder that no matter what happens she has a right to make her own decisions. Her parents don't own her, and neither do her in-laws and her husband. If she wants a job I'll help her get one. If she wants to finish school I'll help with that too. That's what we NGOs are for. This is her life and she needs to live it the way she wants. Now I'll just be a second, darrling, hold on." Her voice trails off.

I place my palm on the mouthpiece and relate Sanjana's advice to Balwinder.

Within seconds I have the necessary information and directions from my friend. I thank her for her help in our need but she dismisses it, saying I'll have to take her to lunch sometime. It's just like being back home.

After hanging up I smile at Didi and Balwinder and give them a hopeful nod. Then I rummage through my handbag for a proper notepad to transfer the information that I'd hurriedly scribbled on the hotel's paper serviette, trying to keep up with Sanjana's pace.

Things To Do:
   1. **Fertility Clinic**
   2. **Police FIR report**
   3. **Bal's confrontation with in-laws**

Within half an hour Balwinder has had her tests at the Hoshiarpur Fertility Clinic. The results are promised for the next morning by a Dr Shalini Singh, who through some good karma of mine has recently returned from New Zealand with her MBBS degree. I build an instant rapport with her. Like a farishta sent from the heavens, she explains the fertility process to both Didi and Balwinder in the easiest possible Punjabi.

Our next stop is the police chowki. "Is it necessary to go to the police?" Balwinder asks, bringing back memories of Tara, the same sort of reluctance in her tone.

"Absolutely! God forbid if they dare try inflicting any harm on you. This way at least there'll be a record with the police that they forced you out of the house. I wouldn't put it past these people to think burning daughters-in-law is as ordinary as having your duppatta tie-dyed!"

More good karma pays off when we come face to face with a lady SSP officer who hates violence against women with a passion. She fills out the FIR report in detail, providing me with a copy for when we're ready for our third mission on the list.

The SSP officer, God bless her, goes the extra mile to write a forceful letter in Punjabi to Balwinder's mother-in-law demanding that she take Balwinder back and learn to respect her son's marriage.

These have to be my first bribe-free experiences in this city in all the time I've been here. I'd always believed in Paulo Coelho's words from his novel *The Alchemist* : "When you want something, all the universe conspires to help you achieve it."

So true.

With my felt-tip pen I place a cross beside numbers one and two of the to-do list. We even have the results of the fertility test. To accomplish the third one I rise from my armchair and give Didi a nod.

She nods back in approval and turns to face Balwinder. "You have to be strong. We have all the proof so you don't have to worry about anything. Come on, let's go."

"Priya Bhabi, how can I ever repay you for this? You don't even know me and already you have done so much," Balwinder says to me, her hands joined together in gratitude.

"Don't mention it. I'm your sister, nah? We all love you, Bal, and if we women don't help each other out then who will? C'mon, don't waste these precious tears now," I say to her with a big, tight hug, my pooh-bear hug I call it, meant only for loved ones.

Some thirty minutes later our Ambassador taxi pulls up in front of a two storey, pale blue house which looks a little like Choudhary Niwas. The nameplate bears the details: Birender Chawla, son of the late Sri

Harnaam Chawla - B.A., LL.B., Adampur.

Balwinder draws in a long breath of strength as she buzzes the doorbell. A tall woman with a thick waist and broad shoulders swivels the door open. Her fair skin appears paler against her beige salwaar kameez and a white chiffon dupatta she wears to cover her grey head. She frowns her big fat nose at Balwinder, its nasal hair enough to have given my late Daada-ji a complex. She glares at Didi and me in disbelief, examining us with rapid eye movements from head to toe and back up again.

"It the kanu aaii tu? Hun ki chaahiye da teinu? Akkal nahi heiga, thawde kol? Hun tussi sada kutch nahi lagdi," she blurts out harshly, demanding to know why Balwinder is back and reminding her that this house and the people in it no longer exist for her.

The woman's loud tone brings another figure to the door, who initially seems pleased to see Balwinder but immediately conceals his elation from the old witch's glare.

I shove my elbow at Balwinder, prompting her to hand over the SSP letter. She nods quickly and holds the letter out to her mother-in-law, who continues to give Balwinder a scornful look.

The witch snatches the sheet of rolled-up paper and dismisses it without opening it, muttering something under her breath about not being able to read English. She gives me a look of contempt as she curses the foreigners who come to this city and pollute the authenticity of her people.

"Punjabi vich likkha hei. Tussi padh lo," I say, instructing her to read the document since it's written in Punjabi.

Grudgingly she unrolls the letter and reads it, her breath becoming louder and puffier, like a dragon ready to blow out fire, as she progresses from one word to another on the page. She hands Birender the letter and he reads it with eyes that narrow in with concern, but slowly his expression turns friendly. He quickly extends his arm towards me and begs us to enter the house.

"Please come in. Relatives don't stand at the door like this. We must arrange for some sewa-satkaar. I'll just send someone to get us some soft drinks and samousas," he pleads, all the while glancing at Balwinder with an "I'm sorry" looks.

Balwinder smiles and motions us to sit on the comfortable cane furniture that is arranged in a large family room.

"Bi-ji," Balwinder says to the old witch, who by now is speechless with shock from reading the threat letter from the police, "please don't do this to me. I'm still your daughter, and you will always be my mother. This is my home, you all are my people and I belong here."

The old witch lowers her eyelids and two symmetrical columns of tears roll down either side of her wrinkled cheeks. "I know, I know, pooth, but I'm sick of everyone telling me that my bahu is a baanjh. How long can I go on suffering people's insults and gossips? Please, please give me a grandson, or even a granddaughter ...I don't mind, just have a child so that everyone can shut up about us being without an heir," she sobs.

Now is a good time to pull stunt number two. If the first stunt - the threat letter - could transform her so much, I wonder what this second one will do.

I glance at Didi and give a little cough, our signal for her to take the cue.

Didi carefully removes the manila folder from her Rupali Fashions plastic bag and hands it to Birender. In the folder are the fertility test results confirming, if I may say so in my Ma's words, that Balwinder's oven is hot and ready to be baked in. That she is not a barren after all.

Dr Shalini Singh had attached a detailed explanation of Balwinder's fertility results in a letter in Punjabi and placed a written request that Balwinder's husband be sent in for a check up as well. She had also enclosed colourful brochures about the clinic and all the services it provides to infertile couples.

After reading and re-reading the letter a few times, the now not-so-bad old woman places her hands over her mouth and weeps with joy. She leaps up from her chair to hug Balwinder with all the energy her sixty year old frame can afford.

A little group hug comprising of the old lady, her son, and daughter-in-law is good enough for Didi and I to sigh with relief and bid them farewell.

In the rickshaw on the way back to the hotel Didi and I chat about her kids and their upcoming end-of-school-year awards day.

"Preetu's growing like a coconut tree, it seems. She can't even fit into the costumes for the gidda dance. Rannu is all excited about playing the part of Shaheed Udham Singh. I'm getting a new kurta-pyjama stitched for him, and his daddy-ji is working on a turban and the beard. He is all excited about the climax scene, practising how he can best shoot his toy pistol at Rahul, the boy who plays General Dyer." Didi's eyes light up a thousand watts when she talks about her kids.

It's great the kids get to learn about such historic events at such an early age. In my time here I have come to observe the fierce passion with which Punjabi children learn about their tragic history, like the Jallianwalabagh massacre that occurred in Amritsar in 1919.

"It's the best way to teach them about their enemies. The young ones need to know the truth."

"Mmm, I don't know about that. I mean, it can backfire in the sense that the kids may grow up with a lot of unjustified prejudice. Why can't people just get over all the British Raj atrocities and the Indo-Pak partition and go on with life? I reckon India is doing so well internationally, what with Bollywood, and all these local millionaires gracing the pages of *Forbes* magazine."

"Still, these English have a lot to answer for. Yes, we're okay with living and letting live but don't ask us to forgive and forget. Okay, maybe forgive but we can never forget. Maybe that's why they are still suffering. They couldn't even let their own princess live in peace. How terrible for her little boys. Lucky she didn't have a girl."

I sense a lightness in her tone. Happy to deviate from the possibly heated debate I say, "They're not little anymore. Will and Harry are very capable young men now and from what I've read they seem to be living up to their mother's dreams. And I think Princess Di would have loved a daughter too."

Didi doesn't look convinced. "Nah, I still feel it was better for her to have only sons. Daughters have a harder time dealing with such loss."

"Hmm, you could be right." I let out a yawn. "Stephanie and Caroline are still dealing with theirs."

"Who?" she asks, bewildered.

"Oh, no one you know." I smile and give her a nudge. Even the street kids know who Diana, Princess of Wales, was but it's a far fetched idea to expect the Monaco Princesse's to have the same fame. We talk some more about the kids, and then the topic changes to the mounting house work since Tara's absence.

"I have an idea." I beam at Didi.

"Please say you're buying me a washing machine." Didi rolls her eyes.

"No, silly. Let's go visit Tara."

Didi freezes half way through her yawn, which I passed onto her. Her mouth remains ajar until an irritating fly lands on her nose, causing her to spit a few times.

"No way. We can't do that, Priya. People will talk."

"So? Let them. Who cares?"

"As a matter of fact, Papa-ji would care. Our status will be in question if he hears from people that his daughters-in-law had sneaked out to visit their former sweeper-girl in jail." Didi hasn't sounded this serious all day. The smile that normally occupies her face is replaced with a serious expression.

"Fine, I'll go then. I can't believe this. This is just getting up to my neck." My right hand swerves up in the air, slicing the invisible particles.

Didi remains silent for a few minutes. The rickshaw driver is also silent, although his silence is probably because he needs to observe the servant-master barrier. He coughs softly every few minutes. The dust rising in the air from passing Maruti cars tickles my throat and I too let out an incessant cough.

Didi places her palm on my back and rubs it gently, forever vigilant of my health.

"Sorry Priya, I didn't mean to growl at you like that."

"It's okay. I need it sometimes." I'm glad she's come off the mute mode.

"You know, I wish I was as courageous as you are," she says. She closes her eyes for a brief moment and takes a deep breath in. The dusty air doesn't seem to have any effect on her India-proof sinuses.

"You are more courageous than you give yourself credit for," I tell her.

She sucks her lips and gazes at me, then shakes her head in negativity.

"I'm serious, Didi. You and each and every woman in this country has an amazing, unbreakable strength. You are survivors. We Westerners think Indian women are submissive, weak. On the contrary, I think you lot prove to be the epitome of contentment and acceptance without expectations. You wake up in the morning smiling, do your chores and never expect rewards. You never question your husband's whereabouts, his intentions. You bear as many children as you are capable of, you cook and clean and wash everyone's dirty laundry. And you still have time for the kids' awards ceremonies. Now, if that's not courage, what is? But in this journey of giving you have placed yourself last in the equation. Didi, you must live life according to your own terms. The operative word here is "live". While your existence revolves around fulfilling everyone else's whims you are putting off living your life. Didi, it's not hard to find that zest for life. It's only difficult when one doesn't already have the inner courage...but you my dear, score ten on ten in that area." I straighten my back and nod, feeling like a motivational speaker.

"I never thought of it that way." Didi squeezes my shoulder. "Thank you for being so nice."

"Anytime, girlfriend." I ruffle the loose ends of her braid.

"Let's go visit Tara," she says.

*****

Of all the places I fantasised about visiting in this exotic country, I never imagined a women's prison to be one of them. I look around the dark, bare, spacious room where the lady officer had asked us to wait. The thought of seeing Tara after so many weeks brings a smile to my face. Didi sits restlessly beside me, mumbling. She elbows me and I realise she has covered her face with her duppatta.

"We should have borrowed a couple of burkhas from someone," she whispers. "I'm about to pee in my pants. All your fault - what if someone here recognises us?"

"Just think how happy Tara will be to see us. She probably hasn't seen a familiar face since she got here."

Just then Tara enters the room accompanied by the same officer. "Ten minutes," says the officer, and closes the door with a loud bang.

Tara runs towards me and hugs me tightly. She embraces Didi and asks about the kids. "I really miss them," she murmurs.

She takes my hands and kisses them. "Memsahib, thank you so much for coming. You don't know how much this means to me. I shall always remember you. I don't know when I will see you all again."

I'm not sure how I am going to go about arranging it but something inside me knows that I will make sure Tara will be a free woman one day. "Don't you worry, Tara, we'll get a good lawyer for you. You will be out of this place in no time. Just have faith and be strong. You'll be free soon."

Tara looks at Didi and smiles and then she holds me. She cups her hands around my face, tears rolling down her bronzed cheeks, and says, "Memsahib, I've never been freer."

The door bangs open and the officer marches in. "Time's up. Chalo."

*****

Back in the hotel room I draw a satisfying line across number three on the list. Facing Didi, I ask her again about the kids. "I miss them like crazy."

But she senses what my heart really wants to know and says, "Gurveer hasn't really been himself. First it's you leaving, then Balwinder showing up like that and being told to go away again." She takes my hands in hers and looks into my eyes. "Priya, ghar chalo, yaar." she begs. *Please come home.*

"No, Didi, I can't go back to a place where my baby is not welcome. I can't let Bi-ji walk all over my life like that. And if Gurveer wants me and his child then he'll have to come to us of his own accord. I'm not going to beg him to choose us."

After holding my grief in for two days I let go. It must be something in Didi's tone or the warmth of her palms that makes the ache in my throat go away and the tears flow freely down my cheeks.

"I understand. So, what now? You can't go on staying here for too long, nah? You've got to make a decision. It's not good for you to be all alone and under so much stress at this stage in your life. You need to relax, Priya, and you need to be around people you can trust and depend on. People who will look after you. As much as I'd give anything to be here with you to take care of you, I'm sorry, my darling sis, I can't. Rannu and Preetu need me, and your Pa-ji too."

"I know, I know, my sweet sweet Didi. I'll figure something out real quick. Don't worry, I'll be fine. Just do me one small favour, no?"

"Name it, das ki chahiyedah, what do you need?"

"I'm craving bhindi sabji so, so, so badly that if I don't eat it for dinner tonight your little niece or nephew here will torture me the whole night with a full blown gymnastics routine!"

"You got it, girlfriend. I'll send a tiffin with Raju in the evening."

Chapter Eight

Decisions, decisions, decisions

Didi's right. I can't go on staying in this beautiful but heartless palace for too long. Though it's only my second night here it feels like I've been in this golden cage for months. I have the keys to get out - all I have to figure out is where I want to fly to.

I lean on the boomerang pillow propped up against the bed head. My stomach is full, thanks to Didi's bhindi sabji with hot chapattis and cucumber and yoghurt raita.

The delicate chrome Pulsar hands revolving on my wrist tell me it's six-forty p.m. Most businesses remain open till eight in this city. Still plenty of time to ring the travel agent. I pick up the phone and politely ask the operator to connect me to Thakur's Travel World. Some twenty seconds later two sharp shrills transmit into my ear, followed by a croaky voice that tells me the person's mouth is chewing onto something as it says in a long drag, "Heeelllloooooooooo?"

"Is that Thakur's Travel World?" I ask, slightly shifting the ear piece a few centimetres from my ear.

"Hanh ji, What I can dooo por you?" says the person, still with his mouth full.

"May I please speak with Mr Talwaar Thakur-Ji?"

"Okay, Madamji, vett van minit pleeees. Talwaar Sar-ji littall bit beee jeey."

"That's fine, I can hold. Please let him know it's Priyanka, Harpal Choudhary's daughter-in-law." It makes me uncomfortable to resort to Papa-ji's name to complete my identity in this instance but I have no choice. Thakur ji is a family friend and has always done the flight ticketing for Gurveer.

Almost immediately after I mention Papa-ji's name a polite gentleman's voice greets me with a pleasant perfect-customer-service tone. It takes almost twenty minutes of polite chat before Thakur-ji keys in my requested departure dates and airline preference and provides a quote, less a standard "Gurveer saab's five percent discount".

I accept the quote and ask him to book a one way passage for me promising to be in his office within the next fifteen minutes with twenty-six thousand, five hundred rupees.

An hour later I call Didi with my flight details "Yes, tomorrow, Didi. Like you said, I can't go on staying in the hotel for long and to be honest, Gurveer has been a real jerk to not even call me in these last two days to see how I am. I mean, what does that say about our love, huh? I really thought he was the one but now…I'm not so sure there is the one out there for people. Besides, you're right, I need to be around people who love me and will care for me - at least I hope they'll love me and look after me."

Didi remains silent for a few seconds, then says, "Gurveer really misses you, you know. He hasn't said much to anyone in the last couple of days and I notice he hardly touches his food. Priya, can I tell him about you going tomorrow? Please, Priya, don't say no."

I don't say yes but I don't say no either. Instead I tell her I'll call her before my taxi leaves for Amritsar International Airport at eight tomorrow morning. I rattle off a list of things that I need her to pack for my trip. She promises to send them over with Raju tonight, and organise to have the remaining items shipped. "And I'll come tomorrow morning. Promise you won't leave without seeing me."

I sit on the giant bed. The room is so full of beautiful things yet so empty. My fingers find the tassels of my duppatta. I twist and pull the loose threads with the same speed as my mind as it races to find answers and justifications for the unplanned agenda of my life. I feel two little jolts in my tummy - "Ouch!" I place my hands on the protruding bit on my tunic and rub it gently. It subsides slowly but two more jolts follow, on the left side now. Definitely a gymnastics routine happening in there.

I fish out Sanjana's card from my handbag and ask the operator to connect me to her number. She is pleased to hear from me again. We chat about Balwinder and how her mother-in-law finally came around. And then I tell her about Tara. She listens in silence during most of it. Finally she asks me about Tara's prison details and promises to try and do as much as she can to help her and her girls. I thank her for being so helpful and for being a good friend.

"Now that I'm your friend, can I ask you something personal?" she asks, taking me by surprise.

"Sure."

"What are you doing away from home in a hotel?"

I tell her everything. Right from the time I met Gurveer to the time I walked out of Choudhary Niwas. I also tell her about my phone call to Ma. "I'm going back to Auckland tomorrow." I swallow the lump in my throat. Something tells me Sanjana knows my eyes are brimming.

"You're doing the right thing, Priya. If there's anything I can do to help, you just need to ask."

"I feel like a total failure," I blurt out.

"Don't be silly. You've been so brave all along. Of course you need to be in a safe and loving environment to have the baby - and let me tell you, that place is not here."

I nod and sniff, using the ends of my duppatta to dab my wet cheeks with. "I just feel I'm running away from the problem instead of solving it. I mean, I'm going back because I can, because I'm a foreigner and I have the means and the passport to enable me to. But what about all those unfortunate women who are helplessly suffering? Having to go through scan after scan and seeing their babies being murdered? They can't just get up and leave like me. I can't help feeling that I'm letting these women down by running away, that I should stay back and battle it."

Priya, you have to do this for your child. God wants you to save this child and that is why you have this golden opportunity that other women don't have. And don't forget these women do have some choices. They may not have a foreign passport to rely on but they certainly have a choice to stand up for themselves. A choice to save their girl child, to take control of their lives. That's where NGOs like ours come in. We can't go knocking on people's doors asking if they are battered and abused. Women need to identify their circumstances and recognise their worth. We are there to help but only if they take the first step to admit that they need that help to regain their identity. To be honest, the ball is in their court just like it is in yours. You have made the best decision for the welfare of your child."

I take in her words of advice and nod in agreement. I thank her again and promise to keep in touch. She mentions Tara once more and says she will start looking into her case straight away.

I place the phone receiver back on its hook and crumble to the floor like a sand castle does when you poke your finger at it. Reality finally hits me. For what seems like hours I sob for the family I will have to leave behind. For Didi, for Rannu and Preetu, for Pa-ji who has been like the brother I never had, for Papa-ji - and surprisingly, even for Bi-ji with her gullibility and naivety. I feel sorry for her more than angry. I cry for Tara. And finally I cry for Gurveer, whom I want with me so badly yet not as badly as I want the best for my child. Our child.

This is my last night in the land I've come to cherish, despite it having so many things that have managed to piss me off. I lie lonesome on this humungous bed, occupying only half of it - my side - as though Gurveer will be lying on his side any moment now. Rubbing my belly gently with one hand, I stretch the other hand over to the bare half of the bed to caress the smoothness of the starched white linen.

My heart skips a beat when I hear the tring tring of the phone, only to realise it's in the next room. Someone must have checked in late this afternoon for there was nobody in it when I came back from Thakur's.

I twist and turn, though not as swiftly as I would like, my growing tummy bubba occupying any space that would usually help me manoeuvre from one side to the other. Still I persist with the slow side-switching, hoping to fall asleep.

I look around the room, hoping to find something to do, something I've left unfinished, so I can kill these last remaining hours. Watching TV is out of the question - there are too many good programmes showing to want to snooze. And there's no more packing to do. Everything is done. Didi made sure that everything Raju brought over in the evening had been arranged neatly in my black Samsonite suitcase.

I told her to keep all my books and ship them over later when things are settled in my life. Who knew where I was to live on a permanent basis? I can't imagine staying with Ma and Pappa for too long. Pouja and I have been victims enough of their fights and their abuse towards each other. I can't let my child get the same raw deal.

I must find part-time employment and do some networking with friends who can mind my baby while I set up a small but comfortable place for us to live in. Perhaps like the little one bedroom place that Gurveer and I had in Howick overlooking the ocean.

With a jolt I sit upright, almost panicking at the realisation that I've forgotten to inform anyone in Auckland about my decision to return. Who can I call without causing a string of questions to erupt? Questions that I'd rather not answer just yet since I'm not sure I know the answers myself.

The only certainty I carry forth with me in returning to my Western home is that I want my baby to be born in a safe, happy, non-sexist environment. Where no one will peer into the delivery room to check on the gender specifics of my child and then tell me how lucky or unlucky I am. An environment where my child will receive proper medical care and immunisation at the required time.

Only one person will listen kindly, and unconditionally agree to receive me at the airport. It is past two a.m. here which means in Auckland, being seven and a half hours ahead, Tammy will probably be getting ready to go to work.

*****

"Wow, babe, that's so great," she squeals with delight as soon as I tell her she'll see me on Wednesday, New Year's Day at eight-thirty p.m. her time.

"No probs, matey, it's grace holiday at work on Thursday so we can stay up all night and chat! I can't wait to see you carrying my little godchild."

I'm right, she doesn't ask me why I'm returning alone and where her "mate Guru" is. We don't speak for long not because she'd be late for the express train, but because I fear I'll tell her the truth, or that she'll notice my voice quivering as I give her my flight details. She hangs up all excited. I hang up confused about what lies ahead.

A little part of me is happy to reunite with my loved ones - especially my non-judgmental friends, Tammy being the number one on that list. I know I can sink into her big bathtub with my big belly and pour my heart out to her while she gives me rosehip tea to sip.

It's three a.m. I can't expect to sleep in the taxi to the airport and I definitely won't be able to sleep in the plane, no matter how comfortable Singapore Airlines is. The seats don't recline far enough and who knows who I'll be sitting next to? I had Gurveer's shoulder to lean on during our thirteen-hour flight from Auckland to Delhi. This time the inflatable pillow must suffice.

If I don't sleep now I'll be a zombie by the time I reach my destination.

Three hours of sleep does me some good. Taking a deep breath, I stretch my arms out of the warm razai and pat my tummy with a hearty yawn. *Hi, you in there.* My tummy bubba is unusually active for such an early hour.

A quick shower and a light tea and buttered toast breakfast later, I decide to flick through today's copy of *Times of India*. The entertainment pages seem like a better way to go this morning, seeing as I don't want to leave India with any more venom in my bile duct than I already have. Besides, I'm thoroughly exhausted from the same old ghisa-pita news about the political hypocrites. At least in the entertainment pages one is transported to the world of fantasy.

Around seven a.m. sharp, the door bell buzzes. Didi's red and green diamante nose stud glints at me as I peep through the door hole.

"Oh, I'm so glad you could make it. I was scared Bi-ji would get suspicious and ask you to do more chores," I say, hugging her tight, resisting the temptation to ask her how Gurveer is and whether or not he knows about me going back to Auckland.

She hugs me back just as tight. "There's no way anyone could have stopped me from seeing you before you leave. Here, take this - it's a little something from your Pa-ji, the kids and me," she says, her voice turning into a slight quiver. She hands me a palm sized burgundy coloured velvet box with Sethi Jewellers written on it in a golden, twirled font.

"Can I open it now?"

"Sure. I hope you'll like it."

"Of course I will."

I unbuckle the square steel hooks. My eyes fill with tears as I find a dainty gold Ganesha pendant and two tiny little sterling silver bracelets with ghungroos on them. The bracelets jingle as I hold them and kiss them, overcome with indescribable emotion. I've never seen such adorable bracelets before.

"The pendant's for you and the bracelets are for our little baby. The jingles will keep all evil eyes away from our darling beautiful child." I like how she avoids using any words that might seem to refer to a boy child.

Hugging her again, I whisper, "Thank you so very much, Didi. These are absolutely beautiful, but you didn't have to."

"Well, too bad, we wanted to and we have every right to. Just because we can't be there for the birth doesn't mean we have no right to spoil our little one. And you." She cries openly now, shedding her suit of armour.

We hold onto each other for several seconds, letting the silence do the necessary I-love-yous, and you-take-cares, and I'll-miss-yous. The silence slowly turns into soft sobs before we finally gather the courage to face the hour of our goodbyes.

As if reading my innermost thoughts, Didi says, "Gurveer and Bi-ji had a very big quarrel yesterday evening after I spoke to you. Ramu confessed to Papa-ji, your Pa-ji and Gurveer that last week Bi-ji gave him five thousand rupees to take to your doctor. After confronting Bi-ji with this truth, Gurveer left. I haven't seen him since, but your Pa-ji told me this morning that he met Gurveer at Mintu's house very early this morning when he went to deliver their milk."

It takes a few moments for her words to sink in. So I was right - Bi-ji wanted to murder my baby if the amniocentesis confirmed I was carrying a girl.

"I don't know what to say, Didi. I love Gurveer and I love you all too. But I love my baby more. I have to do this. I need to do this. I hope some day Papa-ji will forgive me, and maybe Bi-ji too will realise that I did the right thing."

She wipes my tears and nods approvingly.

The receptionist from the lobby phones to let me know my taxi has arrived. I thank her and ask for the bellhop to please come up to collect my bags.

With the last piece of my luggage out of sight, I look around the spacious room to check for any signs of forgetfulness on my part. Lately I've been experiencing more of two things - bladder incontinence and short-term memory loss. It's too difficult to keep track of how many times I have to go to the toilet. Each time my tummy bubba does gymnastics and lands on my bladder it gives me a tingling sensation. Unfortunately it's never any more than a lousy one or two drops of pee that comes out. Technically the bladder is quite empty but the sensation is too ticklish to ignore. And the short-term memory loss is a real pain - I've even started mixing my TV serial plots with each other.

Inspecting the bathroom for the last time and running my palm under the pillows on the bed, I'm satisfied I haven't left anything behind. Rummaging through my handbag, I check to see if I've got my passport and the white and navy striped airline ticket. Yes, they lie tied together with a rubber band, flat in my document pouch.

"Got everything?" Didi asks.

"Yup, I guess so."

The same receptionist who checked me in checks me out, graciously slipping the electronic card key back into the room number slot. She smiles at me and gives me some papers to sign that tell me I owe this palace another two thousand rupees for the numerous phone calls and room service. I pay her cash as Didi frowns and shakes her head, annoyed at being unable to bargain in this situation.

Handing me my payment receipt stapled onto a "With Compliments" slip and a packet of pista badaam, the receptionist thanks me for my stay and wishes me a safe flight. Gee, news travels fast around here - I don't remember telling her I was catching a flight!

Outside, the young chap who took us to the Golden Temple stands, arms folded, next to the taxi - this time a silver Tata Indica hatchback. He has already placed my luggage in the boot. After greeting me with a polite nod he gets into the driver's seat and awaits my instructions.

Didi gives my belly a soft pat and says, "Come and see us soon, bubba. Don't forget your Tai-ji okay?" She kisses my forehead and blesses me with a safe journey and a healthy delivery. "Call me when you get there, okay?"She climbs onto the cycle rickshaw that has been waiting for her and soon becomes a distant figure merging with the morning traffic and the specks of semolina-coloured dust that are gradually clouding the air that had been dustless an hour ago.

I politely ask the taxi driver to wait for a minute. My feisty little gymnast makes me want to go to the toilet again and I'd rather use the hotel's modern English designed one than stop on the way to use a roadside eatery squatting-style pit.

At least I'm wearing loose-fitting jeans and not a salwaar kameeze, which makes the whole process of using the loo so much more difficult - undoing the naadha of the salwaar pants, and then folding up the kameeze top so it doesn't get caught in the seat, and of course there's always the fumbling with the duppatta on the shoulders.

After emptying my bladder and briefly inspecting my reflection in the mirror, I make my way out.

As I approach the revolving glass doors of the hotel entrance/exit, my eyes immediately recognise him in his Lee Cooper faded jeans and my favourite high-necked chocolate coloured Colorado sweater that I bought him from Botany Downs on his birthday, the first one he had after meeting me.

I want to run and hold him tight and beg him to come with me. Instead my feet remain firmly planted to the hand woven Persian foyer rug underfoot. He sees me. I see him. Between us the trio of glass shards revolve, throwing my reflection his way and his my way. Between us is my growing belly, the kicks and punches growing intense, as if my tummy bubba is gleeful at the sight of the father.

Gurveer opens his arms wide and runs in my direction like a hero in a Hindi film. I quickly enter into and exit out of the glass tri-chakra. Before I can show any signs of emotion to him - anger, joy, relief, hard-to-get-ness, or anything - he wraps me tight in his arms. So tight it's as if he'll never let me go, tears rolling down his cheeks and relief erupting in his smile.

He kisses me hurriedly, for the first time not giving a damn about any passers-by, or hotel staff, or the taxi driver, all probably staring at this open-air display of Western style passion. His soft kisses land on my forehead, my cheeks, eyelids, fingers and finally, bending down, he kisses my belly.

"O meri jaan, please forgive me," he says. " I was such a fool to not believe you. Forgive me, jaan please, I beg you."

A woman's heart must be made of salt, I tell myself, for though she may lash out bitter words at her man, his one teardrop is all it takes to melt the crystals. And though her bickering drives him mad sometimes, like food with added salt she adds flavour to his life.

I kiss him back, equally oblivious to the world around us, and stroke his hair and stubbled cheeks. "What took you so long?" I whisper. "We were waiting," I add, resting my hand on top of his, on my belly.

"I was busy organising some stuff," h says coyly.

"Oh yeah? Like what?"

"Like this." He pulls out a white envelope

displaying the twirled words "Thakur's Travel World". He rips it open and unfolds a Singapore Airline ticket bearing the same flight details as mine.

"Trust Thakur-ji to be confidential about his client's flight information," I tease.

Gurveer opens the back door and helps me in the car before sliding in beside me. With one arm around me and his lips full on mine, he taps on the front seat headrest with his other hand. Understanding the signal, our driver begins to rev the engine for the journey ahead.

Epilogue

It's been sixteen months since Gurveer and I returned to Auckland. Each day we wake up to the soft cooing of Pallavi Preet, our daughter, who is now all of twelve months. She is already walking, and the silver bracelets Didi gifted us jingle on her chubby wrists as she waves her arms around gleefully each time she takes those precious tiny steps.

I can hear her shrill laughter in the lounge room as her Papa tickles her tummy. I wipe away the last of the grimes from the oily curry left on the aluminium rims of the stove. Soon we're heading off for the airport to receive Papa-ji, Bi-ji, Didi and the kids.

They're coming to visit us for a month while Pa-ji, who has finally settled down minds the dairy farm.

After leaving India Gurveer and I didn't know where we stood in relation to mending things with his mother. Gurveer had left after the bitter confrontation about the five thousand rupees she'd paid Dr Siddhu to get rid of our baby if it was a girl, and in New Zealand ceased all contact with his parents.

But when the warmth of our daughter's newborn body touched our arms it mellowed our hearts. We rang Gurveer's parents and shared our joy with them.

Bi-ji's endless apologies were accepted with tears of joy from us. Blessings were bestowed, apologies were exchanged and accepted, and love resonated through the phone lines.

All in all, a happy Choudhary household.

Weekly telephone calls and monthly jiffy-bags containing Pallavi's photos have kept them updated about her first smile, her first ba-ba and dah-dah, her first sitting-up-on-her-own, and her first step.

I've also kept in touch with Sanjana through weekly emails, each mail strengthening our friendship, just as I'd hoped. Sanjana is currently working with a lawyer for Tara's freedom from prison and has kept Tara's daughters and niece in a reliable foster home awaiting Tara's release.

Balwinder's good news arrived in my post box last month. She is expecting - and no, her mother-in-law is not going to make her drink any strange milk drink at four a.m. for seven mornings, and nor is she going to force her to go for an amniocentesis test.

Tammy is in love, but first she wants to go trekking in Spain. "Love can wait for two months, or maybe he can turn up in Seville and propose," she told me at the airport.

Daksha Auntie still needs to lose weight and monitor her sugar intake. Shanta-Ben Kaki and Bilas Kaka prefer Toronto's cold winters to Auckland's rains. "Thank God," Ma quipped after hanging up from Shanta Kaki's phone call.

My Patel folks are still quirky - Ma still submissive and Pappa still a promiscuous, stingy scrooge. Pouja, probably the smartest of the lot, flashes a two carat-diamond on her ring finger, courtesy of the much older "Kiwi boy". Salesh is in puppy love with Anna Lee, his class-mate.

I guess all in all, a happy Patel household too.

The End

@ Princess R Lakshman, 2007

Author's Note

This book was inspired by many real life events that occur in lives of women in India. One such unfortunate event is female foeticide. At least one girl child is murdered every day in India. Many women willingly choose to turn a blind eye at this sinful act. They continue to live as murderers of their girl foetuses. If you know anyone who is involved in committing or promoting this unforgivable act, please do the right thing and report the matter to the police.

Save the girl child.